The chill of the evening air bit through the thick fog. Darkness began to surround Chris and Steve.

Suddenly, Chris let out a terrible cry of excitement and fear. He pointed out over the loch and tried to speak. But nothing came out except choking gasps. Finally, he was able to blurt out, "W-w-what's that over there?"

Steve squinted in the direction his cousin was pointing. Suddenly, he felt like his breath was sucked right out of him.

Shadow Over Loch Ness

by Jason Steele

cover illustration
by Richard Kriegler

To David and Nancy—
may your adventures always be unlimited

Published by Worthington Press
801 94th Avenue North, St. Petersburg, Florida 33702

Copyright © 1990 by Worthington Press,
a division of PAGES, Inc.

Printed in the United States of America

10 9 8 7 6 5 4 3 2

ISBN 0-87406-498-8

One

"AAAAAGH!"

Chris Mansfield's scream split the quiet night.

The scream awakened Steve Ridgley, Chris's cousin. Steve jumped out of bed and ran over to where Chris was sleeping.

"Chris, wake up!" Steve said as he shook his cousin.

"No! No! No!" Chris mumbled as he fought off an invisible attacker.

Steve watched his big, blond-haired cousin toss around in the small bunk bed. Chris was already over six feet tall and he wasn't even in the tenth grade yet. Even though the boys were the same age, Steve was small by comparison. They didn't look like cousins—Steve was Vietnamese. He'd been adopted by Chris's aunt when the boys were only three years old.

Chris screamed again. Steve turned on the

lamp next to Chris's bed and tried to wake his cousin again. This time, Chris woke up, squinting into the glaring light at Steve.

"Oh, man," Chris said. His voice was groggy. "That dream was bad." He leaned up on his elbow and shook his head.

"It must have been pretty weird. Even when we were little kids you didn't get freaked out like that," Steve said.

"It was really strange. I was in a little boat or canoe, out on this big lake."

"Like the lake in the picture in your dad's office?" Steve asked.

"I don't know, maybe," Chris said sleepily.

"So what else happened?"

"It was really quiet, too quiet, like something was going to happen. But nothing did, that's what was so scary," Chris said quietly.

"That's it?"

"No, suddenly I saw this huge shadow hanging over me. But I couldn't see what was making it. I only saw this terrible, dark shadow."

"And that's when I woke you up?" Steve asked. His voice sounded loud in the quiet room.

Chris hesitated. He shivered and then continued softly, "No. I finally saw this long-necked thing towering over me. And I was just waiting, waiting for it to strike."

"Let's go downstairs to your dad's office and look at that picture again," Steve suggested.

"Ah, I don't want to look at it again," Chris protested.

"Come on," Steve said, pulling his cousin's arm.

They tiptoed down the creaky, old stairs. Chris and his dad, Paul Mansfield, had lived in the big, rambling house in the Ohio countryside ever since Chris's parents had divorced. Steve lived in nearby Columbus, but he often visited his cousin during the summer when school was out.

The boys walked into the office and Steve flicked on a table lamp. Its light cast strange shadows on the unusual souvenirs and strange objects that covered one wall. The African witch doctor's mask seemed to flash its hideous grin at the boys. A gigantic great white shark's tooth and a pair of Cheyenne tomahawks seemed ready to attack.

The room was the office of Adventure Unlimited, Chris's dad's company. The company took tourists on fantastic adventure trips all over the world. One whole wall was a world map with little pins marking the places where Adventure Unlimited had traveled. Whenever the trips were in the summer, the boys got to go along.

Steve walked over to the wall with the

souvenirs. There, between a voodoo doll and a coiled, stuffed cobra, was a small framed drawing. Steve took it off the wall and handed it to Chris. They walked over to the table with the lamp on it and looked at the drawing for the thousandth time.

It was an etching, its black ink faded with age. The picture was dated 1799 and it showed a lake surrounded by cliffs. The sky above the lake was filled with threatening, dark clouds. On top of the cliff, hanging out over the dark lake, perched an ancient stone ruin of a castle or fort.

But the thing that drew their attention was down below the cliff, in the middle of the lake. Rising mysteriously out of the water was the head and long neck of some kind of creature. Its head looked a little like a seal's, but its body and neck were long and snakelike. Its flippers broke the surface of the water.

"That's it, all right," said Chris. "That's what the shadow in my dream looked like."

The boys gazed at the ancient drawing. The old house creaked and groaned around them, and outside the wind blew through the trees. The strange drawing held them under its odd spell.

Just then they heard footsteps in the hallway.

"What's that?" Steve asked in a whisper.

"I heard sounds in here," said a voice. "What are you guys doing up? It's 2:00 in the morning."

Paul Mansfield, a tall, bearded man with blond hair, wearing sweatpants and a Cleveland Browns sweatshirt, walked into the room carrying a piece of paper.

"Hi, Dad," said Chris. "You kind of surprised us. I had a nightmare and couldn't sleep. We came down here to look at the drawing of the monster again."

"Maybe you're just a little nervous about going to Scotland tomorrow," Paul said.

"Maybe. Hey, what are you doing up, Dad?"

Paul walked over to the boys. "Well, I couldn't sleep either. Something kind of weird has happened," he said, pointing to the drawing. "Have I ever told you how I got this?"

"Nope," Chris said.

"When I was in college," Paul began, "I got to know a girl named Fiona Macgregor. She was an exchange student from Scotland. We became pretty good friends and went out a few times. I haven't seen her since college. When she left to go back home at the end of the school year, she gave me this picture. It had been in her family for years and she wanted me to have it to remember her by.

9

I've had it ever since."

"Wait a minute," Steve said. "Isn't the castle where we'll be staying called Castle Macgregor?"

"Uh-huh," Paul said, nodding his head. "Castle Macgregor has been Fiona's family home for hundreds of years," said Paul, stroking his blond beard. "The oldest parts of it were built in the 1400s. Her family is an old Scottish noble family. Her cousin, Duncan Macgregor, is the *laird* of the castle."

"What does that mean?" Chris asked.

"That's the Scottish word for *lord*, isn't it, Uncle Paul?" Steve piped in.

"You're right, Steve. Duncan is the lord of the castle. He's older than Fiona and from what she tells me he's a little unfriendly at first."

"You know what, Steve? Dad was telling me the other day that there are legends about the castle—lots of cool, creepy stuff about ghosts and phantom bagpipers and mysterious knocks on doors and long-lost treasure."

"Here we go again. Chris the Dreamer starts cooking up these stories about ghosts and lost treasure," Steve said.

"At least I don't wear a camera around my neck twenty-four hours a day," Chris replied.

"That's enough, you two," Paul said. "What's with these nightmares, Chris? Do you think you're going to be able to handle this trip?"

"No sweat, Dad," Chris replied. "I don't know why I'm having these dreams. I guess it's just from looking at this creepy picture over and over again."

"You're not the only one interested in that picture," Paul said. "I got this letter from Fiona today and she asked me if I still had the picture."

"Does she still want us to come?" asked Chris.

"Yeah. There's no problem about that. She's been nagging me to bring a tour group to Loch Ness for years." Paul paused and shook his head. "It's the second part of the letter that I don't get. She wants me to be sure to bring the picture of the monster."

"Why?" asked Steve.

"She doesn't say why," Paul explained. "She just says she's sorry to have to ask for it back but to be sure to bring it with me." He brushed his hand through his hair and sighed. "This just doesn't sound like the Fiona I used to know."

Paul stared at the picture for a little while longer. Then he handed the picture to Chris. "My suitcase is already too crammed. Can you put this with your stuff, Chris?"

"Sure, Dad. But the only place I have any

room is in my backpack."

"Just wrap it up in a sweatshirt or something so it doesn't get broken."

"Your backpack is so old and junky everything's probably going to fall out of it over the Atlantic Ocean," Steve teased.

"It's better than—"

Paul interrupted. "Come on, you two. It's almost 2:30 in the morning. You don't want to miss our flight in the morning, do you?"

"No way!" Chris answered. The boys headed out of the room and started up the steps.

"Good night, Uncle Paul," Steve called out.

"Sleep well, guys," Paul answered. "I'll be up in a minute."

Paul walked over and sat down at his big desk. As the boys climbed the stairs, they saw Paul rereading the letter in the pale lamplight. He was frowning and shaking his head.

"Dad looks really worried," Chris said.

"He almost looks scared," Steve added.

"But why would he be scared?" asked Chris.

"I'm not sure. I think it has something to do with the etching."

"Or Castle Macgregor. It sounds like this trip might be, I don't know, dangerous," Chris said.

"Yeah," Steve agreed. "This time I think you're right."

12

Two

THE late afternoon sun was beginning to dip below the Scottish mountains as the rented van bumped over the rough road toward the castle. The six tourists in the group were busy talking and pointing at various sights. But Chris and Steve sat silently. Each boy had the same thing on his mind—the mysterious monster of the loch. Would they see it? Would they meet anyone who had? What was it, exactly? Where had it come from? And if it *was* a prehistoric monster, how had it survived all of these years?

"Look!" one of the tourists shouted, breaking into Chris and Steve's thoughts. "There it is! Castle Macgregor!"

Steve and Chris looked out the window of the van.

Looming at the far end of an open field, rising above the trees on a high, rocky cliff, was a large, gray stone building with tall towers. It was surrounded by a low wall. "It's awesome!" whispered Chris to his cousin. "It's a real castle, just like I pictured it."

Steve just stared out the window at the gloomy castle as the van made its way up the winding road. They drove through a gate and pulled up in front of Castle Macgregor.

Chris and Steve scrambled to the front of the van so that they could be the first ones out. Paul looked at them sternly. "Hey guys, take it easy. The Loch Ness monster isn't going anywhere!"

But the boys pushed out ahead of the rest of the passengers anyway. As the tourists began to sort through their suitcases, Chris and Steve looked around them. Even though it was late afternoon, the entire countryside had a dark, creepy look about it. It was easy to believe that an ancient monster—or something far worse— haunted the dreary countryside. Suddenly, Chris and Steve heard an eerie sound floating down from somewhere above them.

"What's that?" Chris asked. "It sounds like some sort of animal, like something inhum—"

Steve interrupted him. "Chris, you wimp. It's just a bagpipe."

Chris cocked his head and listened. The sound was haunting. The bagpipe's lonely, far off wail seemed to pierce through the chilly, late afternoon air.

"Well, it's still spooky anyway," Chris said. "Remember what I was telling you about the phantom bagpiper?" Chris asked his cousin in a low voice. "And besides, I can't see where it's coming from, can you?"

"It must be coming from someplace up there," Steve said, pointing up toward the tallest tower.

As Chris searched the tower walls for a sign of the bagpiper, his eyes fell on a third-floor window. Its curtain was pulled slightly open. He nudged his cousin and said in a low voice, "Don't look now, but I think we're being watched."

Steve gazed up at the window. There, behind the curtain, was a man's face, stern and unsmiling. The man's eyes seemed to bore right into them. Both boys stared back for a second at the mysterious man behind the curtain. Then, as quickly as he had appeared, he vanished.

Chris caught his cousin's eye for a second. Steve pulled his jacket tighter around his neck, as if something besides the chilly air was making him shiver.

The sound of the bagpipe was interrupted by another sound—the sound of a woman's voice. Chris and Steve looked toward the voice. A tall, dark-haired woman was standing in front of the castle door.

"Paul!" she shouted, her arms outstretched. "I'm so happy to see you. It's been a long time!"

Even from a distance, Chris could tell that his father was smiling broadly. Chris and Steve watched as Paul took Fiona into his arms and hugged her warmly. Finally, Paul broke their embrace and motioned for the boys to join them.

"Chris, Steve, everyone, I'd like you to meet Fiona," Paul said, smiling. Then he quietly added, "My old friend."

"Welcome to Castle Macgregor, Adventure Unlimited!" Fiona said to the group. "I hope that you'll have the adventure of your lives here! I'm so glad you're finally here." Fiona looked at Chris and Steve. "Chris, you look just like your dad . . . when he was younger, that is," she said, winking at Paul.

Fiona led the group through the castle's massive wooden doors into the parlor.

"I like her," said Chris to Steve as they watched Fiona greet each of the six guests individually.

"Yeah, and I think your dad does, too," Steve said as he elbowed Chris in the ribs. "She's pretty. Hmm . . . maybe they could get married and you could settle down here, learn to play the bagpipes . . ."

"Knock it off, sub-humanoid," muttered Chris.

Before Steve could reply, Fiona announced that she would lead the guests to their rooms. As they were climbing the stairs to the third floor, Steve nudged Chris and nodded toward a closed door at the end of a hallway. "That has to be the room where the man we saw was standing."

"Boys," Fiona interrupted, "your room is there, at the end of the hallway." She motioned toward the door that Steve had just pointed out to Chris.

"But, uh, but . . . ," Chris managed to say.

Steve jumped in. "We're not putting anyone out or anything, are we? I mean, we could sleep anywhere really."

Fiona gave the boys a puzzled look then laughed. "Does it look like we're short of space here? Of course, these rooms haven't been occupied for years. We had to do a lot of cleaning just to get them ready for Adventure Unlimited."

Steve and Chris headed reluctantly toward the room at the end of the hall.

Chris reached for the door. "You don't suppose whoever we saw is still in there, do you?"

"There's only one way to find out, wimp," Steve said as he reached past Chris and opened the door.

The room was filled with furniture that looked like it was about a hundred years old, maybe even more. There was a huge bed, with a wooden, carved headboard.

"See, Chris," Steve said, "there's no one here."

Chris looked around the room. He even stooped to check under the bed, but he didn't see anyone.

"Hey. Quit spooking yourself and check this out!" Steve said, pointing to the window. "We can see the loch from here!"

Chris hurried to the window where Steve was standing. He could barely make out the lake in the distance.

The boys stared out across the fields toward Loch Ness. They felt drawn to it, as if by magic. They couldn't take their eyes off the distant, silvery water.

They were both quiet for awhile, thinking their own thoughts. Finally Chris said in a low voice, "I wonder if there's anything out there. With all the legends and all the sightings, you almost have to think there's *something* out there."

"It's really weird actually being here,"

added Steve. "Doesn't it feel kind of creepy, knowing we're so close to it—whatever it is? Some people think it's a dinosaur that's survived all these years—somehow."

"Well, if dinosaurs could survive anywhere, it'd be up here. It feels like nothing has touched this place for years."

"Hey, what's that stone thing way out there? It looks like a building or something."

"I don't know," Steve answered. "We can take a look tomorrow."

"Are you kidding? Wait until tomorrow? Who's the wimp now?" asked Chris. "Let's take a look right now."

Suddenly, there was a loud knock on the door of their room. Both boys jumped.

"Who's there?" called Chris.

A voice called out something in a heavy Scottish accent. The boys looked at each other and shrugged their shoulders. Then they jumped up and opened the door just in time to see a gray-haired man start down the steps at the end of the hall. They could hear the man mumbling something over and over as he shuffled down the stairs.

Chris scratched his head. "Did you understand what he said? That accent was so thick I couldn't understand a thing."

Steve bent his body over a bit and imitated

the old man. "Cam don ta the dinnin rum. Teem farrr dennar averyone."

Chris laughed. "It sounded like something about dinner. At least I hope so. I'm pretty hungry."

Chris looked toward the open window. The mysterious loch and the stone building sure looked tempting. His stomach grumbled. "I guess we'll have to go take a look tomorrow. We wouldn't want to miss 'dennar'!"

Steve and Chris headed down the hallway to the castle's huge dining room. The walls were covered with big, old tapestries that showed hunting scenes. A glittering chandelier hung from the high ceiling and silver candlesticks ran down the center of the long table.

All the guests had assembled around the table, and Chris and Steve sat down in two of the three empty chairs that were left. They noticed that the chair at the head of the table was empty.

Fiona stood up and welcomed them. Then she introduced the short, powerful-looking, blond-haired man with a small mustache who was sitting next to her.

"This is Captain James Ross, retired from the British army," Fiona explained. "He's going to be your guide while you're here. He grew up in the Highlands and I'm sure he'll

20

be able to answer all your questions."

Captain Ross smiled and nodded as the guests clapped.

"Where's the laird?" whispered Chris to Steve.

Steve was about to answer when a deep voice behind them said, "Please accept my apologies for being late."

A tall, dark-haired man of about fifty walked quickly into the dining room and took the empty chair. He looked around the table at all the guests. His eyes lingered for a moment on Steve and Chris.

Steve and Chris gasped at the same time.

It was the man at the window.

The boys noticed that he made eye contact with Fiona for an instant. The look he gave her wasn't a friendly one.

"I am Duncan Macgregor," he said quietly. "Welcome to Castle Macgregor."

Chris and Steve noticed the guests looking around the room. Maybe they weren't the only ones who had noticed the tension between Fiona and her cousin.

"Well," said Paul quickly, "why don't we all introduce ourselves?"

The guests started talking and the tension left the room. As they ate dinner, Captain Ross told some pretty funny jokes about

Scottish people and Fiona told the group some history about the castle and the Loch Ness area. Paul outlined their schedule for the week. Duncan said nothing, but he seemed to be listening to everything. His dark eyes kept moving around the table.

After dinner, Fiona announced that the group would have coffee in the drawing room. "Angus, our groundskeeper, has started a nice, big fire, so we'll all be very comfortable. It can be very chilly up here in the Highlands."

"That's right," added Captain Ross. "The calendar might say spring, but you wouldn't know it tonight!" He laughed his good-natured laugh, one the boys had heard lots of times at dinner.

"Let's go outside," whispered Chris. "It's too dark to find our way to the loch, but we can do some exploring around here. Maybe we'll find someone who's at least seen the monster."

The boys got their jackets and found their way out into the yard of the castle. They walked around under the castle walls, peeping into small buildings and listening to the sounds of the night. The castle grounds seemed deserted.

"It's really dark," said Chris.

"Yeah. I think the moon'll be rising pretty soon."

"How would you know that?"

"I read in my travel almanac that it would," answered his cousin.

"I swear, your brain is too big for your own good."

"Hey, if you ever want to borrow any of it, just let me know."

"Look at that," Chris said, pointing to a light in a small building at the far end of the castle yard. "Let's check it out." Their shoes crunched loudly on the gravel as they walked toward the building. They stepped into the doorway and heard a horse whinny, then another.

"Hi. Anybody here?" called Steve.

"Aye, come in, laddies." It was the same voice they had heard at their bedroom door before dinner.

Steve and Chris stepped into the stable. The warm smell of horses and hay tickled their noses. In the light they saw an old, but powerful-looking man spreading straw around the horse stalls. He was wearing a kilt, the traditional skirt-like garment worn by Scottish men for centuries.

"Angus is me name. Angus Campbell," said the man as he continued to spread straw.

"I'm Chris Mansfield and this is my cousin Steve Ridgley."

"He must be the one who called us for

dinner," Steve whispered when the man turned to get more straw.

"Yeah. It's easier to understand him when we're talking to him face to face," Chris added.

"Umm, Fiona said you were the grounds-keeper here, Mr. Campbell," Steve said, trying to make conversation.

"Call me Angus, laddie."

"Okay, Angus."

"I've been working here at Castle Macgregor for seventy-two years," the old man explained. "My father was servant to the laird's father and my grandfather was servant to his grandfather."

Steve and Chris looked at each other.

"Umm, have you ever seen the Loch Ness monster?" Chris asked.

The old man looked at them and, for the first time, a hint of a smile came to his face. He shook his head. "Never in seventy-two years," he answered. "And I never expect to see it. I think the whole thing is nothing but legends and stories. The winters are long up here and many people have nothing better to do than start making up stories about a monster of some kind in the loch."

"Oh," said Chris, unable to hide his disappointment.

"But," continued Angus, "I know people

who don't think it's just legends and stories. And some of them are smart folks. If they say they've seen something, then maybe there is something to it after all. All I can say is that *I've* never seen the creature. If you ask me, there are enough strange things that have happened here over the years without a monster in the loch."

"Yeah? What kind of strange things?" asked Chris with a gleam in his eye.

Angus leaned on his pitchfork. "Well, laddies, these castle walls have seen their share of murders and killings. The laird's great-great-great grandfather was murdered on the shores of Loch Ness, right out by the old fort. Some say his own cousin did it, but they never found out for sure."

"His own cousin?" asked Chris.

Angus nodded. "And then there's the ancient Macgregor family treasure that disappeared after the Rebellion. The family wanted to hide it from the English soldiers who were prowling the Highlands. Whoever hid it did a good job, because it's been lost ever since."

"Was it a big treasure?" Steve asked.

"Aye, that it was. The laird at that time wanted to keep everything from falling into the hands of the English army. The soldiers took him away to be hanged for his part in the Rebellion, but no one ever found the treasure."

"What's this Rebellion?" asked Chris.

"In the 1700s, the Scottish Highland families fought several times against the English—the last time under Bonnie Prince Charlie, the guy they wanted to be king," explained Steve. "The Scottish lost and the English took away almost everything. A lot of families had to give up their old ways of life."

Angus smiled at Steve, his bright eyes shining. He nodded and said in a low voice, "It sounds like you know a wee bit about our ancient Scottish history, lad."

Steve looked embarrassed. "A little," he answered. "I read a book on it before we came."

"He knows a wee bit about everything," said Chris, shaking his head.

In the eerie darkness, the boys listened to the old man's voice as he talked about what had happened a long time ago. The cold wind was blowing through the cracks in the stable's ancient walls. It was almost like the things he was telling had just happened yesterday, not hundreds of years ago. The boys shivered.

"There's another legend you might hear something about since you're interested in that monster in the loch," continued Angus. "People talk of a phantom bagpiper who is heard far away on moonlit nights. And whenever he's heard, people say that it means the Loch Ness monster is about to appear, bringing misfortune and bad luck to the castle and to the Macgregor family."

The boys were silent. The only sound they heard was the haunting, melancholy hooting of an owl off in the distance.

"Well, do you think the story is true?" asked Chris after a while.

Angus shrugged his shoulders and answered with a strange smile on his face, "Who am I to say? This is a lonely corner of the world, and strange things happen in lonely places. Terrible, unexplained things," he said, shaking his head.

"Uh, maybe it's time to go back inside," said Steve in a low voice. "They'll be wondering where we are." The boys turned to leave.

"I'll tell ye, laddies," said Angus as they were heading out the door. "Since you're so interested in this monster, you might want to talk to Mary, me wife. She's the cook here at the castle." In the light of the lantern, they could see a twinkle in Angus's eye.

"Okay," answered Chris. "But why should we talk to her?"

Angus smiled. "Because she claims to have seen the monster, that's why! Now, goodnight, laddies. You may want to talk to Mary in the morning."

Chris and Steve ran back to the front door of the castle.

"Do you believe that?" asked Chris. "Awesome! I can't believe we're going to get to talk to someone who's seen the monster!"

"You mean someone who *says* she's seen the monster," said Steve, as the boys entered the front door of the castle.

"Let's go say good night to everyone," said Steve. "It's been a pretty long day and I'm beat. Besides, I want to get up early and check out all those stories."

"I have to tell Dad about the cook seeing the monster," said Chris.

They stood at the door of the drawing room and watched the guests, who were gathered in small groups, laughing and talking. Fiona and Paul were sitting apart from the others, in front of a roaring fire, talking in hushed tones, their eyes looking straight at each other.

"Chris, do you think we should bother them? They look kind of busy," Steve said.

But Chris was already heading to the cozy place by the fire where Fiona and Paul were sitting. Steve just shook his head and followed.

"Dad! We talked to someone who knows someone who has seen the Loch Ness monster! Angus says that his wife Mary has actually seen it!"

Paul smiled. "Or at least she thinks she did," he answered with a laugh.

"Speaking of the loch," Fiona said, her face becoming serious. "Paul said that you brought the etching of the castle and the monster."

"Yeah," answered Chris. "It's upstairs in my backpack."

"If it didn't fall out of that grungy, old thing," added Steve. Chris gave him a dirty look.

"I'm sure Paul told you I'm very anxious to have it back," she said. "It means a lot to me."

"Well," said Chris, "we were just going to bed now, but I'll bring it down at breakfast tomorrow."

Fiona hesitated for a moment and then answered, "Of course, that's fine. I'm sure it's safe. You can just give it to me tomorrow morning."

"Okay," said Chris.

The boys said good night and climbed the stairs to the third floor. They saw through a window on the landing that the moon had risen. It looked almost full.

Climbing into their beds, the boys talked for a bit about the monster, about what it could be, and about what kinds of questions

29

they would ask Mary. But they were so tired from the trip and the excitement they were both asleep before they knew it. Even the bright moon shining in the window couldn't keep them awake.

Sometime in the middle of the night, Steve, who was a light sleeper, heard a sound in the room. Thinking it was probably a mouse or a bird at the window, he turned over. But then he heard it again. It sounded like things being moved around quietly. He cautiously opened his eyes.

The moon had set again, so the room was dark. But over in the corner, where they had dropped their backpacks, a figure was kneeling and carefully lifting things out of a pack.

"Hey!" shouted Steve.

In an instant, the figure stood up and dashed from the dark room. It all happened so fast that when the figure was gone, Steve couldn't tell if he had dreamed the whole thing or if the incident had actually happened.

"W-what's going on?" mumbled Chris, waking up.

"There was someone in here," his cousin answered. "At least I-I think there was. I'm going to turn on the light."

The light blinded them for a few seconds.

When their eyes finally adjusted, they hopped out of bed and ran to where the packs were lying.

"Someone was here, all right," whispered Steve, kneeling down. "I didn't just dream it. Someone's been looking through our stuff." He got up and looked out into the hallway, but there was no one there. He shut the door and came back to the packs.

"I don't get it," said Chris, shaking his head. "This is too weird. Maybe we should go get Dad."

"No, let's just lock the door from now on. We'll tell him tomorrow morning."

Chris headed to the big, wooden door and turned the lock.

"Hey, Chris," whispered Steve, "you know how I'm always teasing you about how your old pack looks like it came from a garbage dump?"

"Yeah. So?"

"Well, if you were a burglar looking for something to steal, wouldn't you look in the nice, new pack to see what was there?"

"I guess so."

"Well, your junky, old pack has been torn apart," said Steve, gazing at his cousin. "Mine hasn't been touched."

31

Three

CHRIS and Steve stared at each other for a minute.

Finally, Chris said, "Why would somebody search through my old pack and not your new one? And look—your camera's sitting right there on the dresser. It would have been an easy steal."

"Check to see if anything's missing from your pack," Steve urged him.

Chris sorted through the jumbled pile of clothes that lay on the floor around his pack. It looked like Steve had woken up before the thief had had much of a chance to go through Chris's pack.

"This is crazy," said Chris. "My wallet and passport are right here on top. Why wouldn't a burglar take them?"

"What else is in there?" asked Steve.

"Nothing really. Just hiking stuff, clothes,

shoes, a few books. I don't get it."

"Wait a minute," said Steve sharply. "Where's the sweatshirt with the picture of the monster in it?"

Chris knew right away what his cousin was thinking. He dug into the bottom of the pack and pulled out his Ohio State sweatshirt. He carefully unwrapped the picture.

"It's okay. But why would anyone want to steal this?" Chris wondered out loud. "It's just a picture."

"Bring it over here in the light," answered Steve. "Let's look at it."

"We've already looked at it a hundred times."

"Well, bring it here anyway. Let's look at it again."

They sat on Steve's bed and examined the old picture one more time. They turned it over and over, hoping to find some clue that might tell them if someone had actually been trying to steal it.

"Shh!" hissed Chris. "Did you hear that? Footsteps! Out in the hall!" He sprang up and walked quickly to the door. It creaked as he opened it. He peered into the dark hallway.

"No one's there," he whispered. "Maybe it was my imagination."

"Yeah, I'm a little jumpy, too," answered Steve. "It's a weird feeling knowing that somebody's been going through your stuff."

They looked at the picture again. Chris held it upside down. Then he held it sideways. Finally, he turned it over in his hands.

"Hmm. Let's bend up those little nails that hold the picture in the frame. The back looks like a separate piece of cardboard or something."

"I don't know. Maybe that will wreck it."

"Don't worry. I'll be careful," answered Chris. "We can put it back together again. Hand me my Swiss army knife."

As Steve watched, Chris worked the knife blade under the nails that held the back of the picture in place. They were rusty and tough to bend, but finally Chris bent the last nail up and carefully lifted off the back.

"Be careful," said Steve. "It's really old. It might crumble."

"Steve! Look at this!" yelled Chris.

"Shhh! Somebody might hear you!"

"There's something written on the back of the picture," whispered Chris. "It was covered up by the backing."

"Can you read it?"

"It's old and faded, but I think I can."

Chris held the back of the picture up to the light of the bedside lamp. They read together. Written in an old-fashioned script were the words:

Where witches burn, beware the Beast,
When moon is full, look to the east.
Above the wolf, below the star,
Turn blood to gold, rip open the scar.

"What does it mean?" asked Steve, after they had read the poem several times.

"I don't know. It sounds like a Halloween poem—witches, the Beast, the wolf, blood. It's pretty strange."

"Those nails were so rusty, I bet no one has looked at the back of this picture for years and years," said Steve.

"Hey, Steve," said Chris, "could this old picture really be what someone wanted to steal? It just doesn't make sense. I mean, who would rob a kid? All of the other guests are a lot richer than us. If I were a burglar, I'd rob that lawyer from San Diego. He's got a $2000 video camera."

Steve nodded, but said nothing.

"Hmm. What are you thinking?" asked Chris, staring at his cousin.

"I'm trying to think logically about this. Let's just suppose somebody did want to steal this picture," said Steve, talking slowly. "Why?"

"Well," said Chris, "because they wanted it, I guess."

"Duhhh," said Steve with a groan. "I know

that. But *why* would the person want it?"

"You tell me, if you're so smart."

"A person would try to steal it because he really liked the picture, or because it was worth a lot of money, or because he thought the picture could tell him something."

"Well, it is a nice picture," said Chris. "But I've seen millions of better pictures. This one's all faded."

"Right. Scratch the first reason."

"And I wonder if this thing is really worth a whole lot of money," Chris said. "I mean, it's old and all, but I don't think it's very rare. It says, 'Printed in Edinburgh, 1799.' That means they must have printed up a lot of them."

Steve smiled and said, "Not necessarily. But you're probably right, Chris. I think there's hope for you yet. Pretty soon you'll be tying your own shoes."

"Hah, real funny," Chris said.

Steve continued, "That leaves the last reason. This thing must have a secret meaning. That must be why somebody would want to swipe it."

"It's got to be the poem," answered Chris, holding up the back of the picture to the light again. "It could have a secret meaning. But we'll never figure it out. It's just a bunch of spooky words." He read the poem out loud again.

"It just doesn't make any sense at all," Chris said.

"Well, let's look at it from another angle," Steve said. "If we know that someone wanted the picture because of the poem, who could the burglar be?"

"Well, we know it wasn't Fiona, because we were going to give it to her in the morning."

"And besides, I think it was a man," added Steve. "I couldn't see very well, but I think it was a guy."

"What else?"

"Well, it seems like the only reason to steal this thing is to read the poem on the back. Right?" asked Steve.

Chris nodded. "So the thief would have to know about the poem on the back. And he'd have to know what it meant, too. Maybe he'd have to know about the history of the castle and the family."

"And he would have to know his way around to be able to sneak in and out like that," added Steve.

Chris stared at his cousin. "There's only one person who fits that description," Chris said.

Steve nodded. "Duncan," he said.

"Well, what are we going to do? We'd better keep an eye on him."

"We'll have to be careful," said Steve. "I think we ought to give the picture to Fiona and tell her about the thief. She's your dad's friend. She'll know what to do. And I don't think she trusts Duncan either. Did you see the way she looked at him at dinner?"

"Yeah, I did. But listen, let's write down the poem before we give it to her. That way we can do some investigating on our own."

"I don't know, Chris. I sure wouldn't want to get on the wrong side of that Duncan guy. Besides, I don't see how we'll ever figure it out. It's like a riddle—a two-hundred-year-old riddle."

Chris shook his head. "Maybe you're right, but we've got to at least try! Someone thought it was important enough to try and steal it. Come on! Who's being the wimp now?"

"It's just that this could be dangerous, that's all."

"Well, we'll just be careful," said Chris.

"All right, all right," Steve said. "Write down that poem and put the picture back together. Then let's get some sleep. It looks like we're going to have more to track down than the Loch Ness monster tomorrow."

* * * * *

The next morning, the room was flooded with sunshine. The gloom and mystery of the previous night seemed unreal. It was hard for both the boys to believe that the attempted robbery had even happened. It all seemed like a strange dream.

After breakfast, the boys caught up with Paul just as he was preparing to take the group on a sightseeing trip to a museum down the loch. They told him everything that had happened. Paul took the boys straight to Fiona. They repeated their story for her.

"Here's the picture," said Chris, handing her the etching. "It'll be safer with you, I guess."

"Thanks," said Fiona, taking the picture and slipping it into her handbag. "I'm really very concerned about someone breaking into your room. Nothing like this has ever happened here. I'm going straight to the police about this. I'll give them a full report. But why would anyone want this so badly he'd be willing to steal it?"

"What about the poem on the back?" asked Steve. "Maybe the burglar wanted to get the poem?"

Fiona seemed surprised. "How did you boys know about the poem?"

"Oh, well, we . . . ," Chris stammered.

Steve helped him out. "Well, we figured out

that someone was after the picture because they didn't take anything of real value. So we took the picture apart to see if we could find out anything more." He looked up apologetically. "I hope you're not mad at us for taking the picture apart. We did put it back together."

Fiona shook her head. "I'm not mad. In fact, I'm glad you told the truth. But I don't think anyone would want the etching for the poem. It's just some children's nonsense or some silly, old spooky legend. Anyway," she added with a shrug, "I'll take care of this. It's not your problem, it's mine. And you're supposed to be on vacation."

"Yeah, come on boys. We're almost ready to leave," Paul added.

"Dad, would you mind if we didn't go this time?" Chris asked. "We didn't get much sleep last night."

"Well, I'm not real happy about leaving you two here," Paul said.

"We'll be all right, Dad. What's going to happen to us in broad daylight? Angus is here, and Mary, and other people, too. Besides, we want to check out the monster," Chris said, winking at Steve.

"Well, okay," said Paul. "Captain Ross is waiting for me with the group at the van. I guess I'll get going. Are you sure you don't want to come with us?"

"We're positive," Chris said.

"All right. But see if you can manage to stay out of trouble while I'm gone."

"Dad, you know us. Would we get into trouble?"

"I know you very well—that's why I'm saying it," Paul said with a smile.

"Come on, Paul," said Fiona. "I'll walk out with you."

Chris and Steve noticed that Fiona slipped her arm into Paul's. Steve raised his eyebrows and whispered to Chris, "Start practicing your bagpipes."

The boys turned to run up the stairs but decided to slow down. They didn't want to look too eager to go exploring. On the first landing, they nearly bumped right into the grim-faced Duncan. He must have been standing on the landing the whole time! *How long had he been there? How much had he overheard? Did he know about the poem?* they wondered.

"Uh, sorry," the boys muttered and ran upstairs. Looking down the polished, wooden railing, they saw the laird's hard, dark eyes looking up at them.

Four

ONCE they were up in their bedroom, Chris watched from the window as the Adventure Unlimited van pulled away. His dad was in the front with Captain Ross. He heard a car door slam and saw Fiona drive off in her car in the opposite direction. He guessed she was probably on her way to the police station.

"Maybe Dad was right," Chris muttered as he gazed out the window.

Steve was staring at the poem they had copied from the back of the etching. He looked up at his cousin. "About what?" he asked.

"Oh, nothing. This place is just getting to me, I guess. Let's get out of this room."

"Great. Where do you want to go first? Do you want to look for the monster?" Steve asked.

"Nah. Let's check out the rest of the castle."

"Okay. But wait a minute. I want to get my camera."

First, they found the stairway to the cellar and started down the dark steps. "This is more like a dungeon than a basement," Chris said.

"Yeah, the only things missing are chains on the walls and instruments of torture."

"The rest of this stuff just looks like junk," Chris said.

"Yeah, let's check out the rest of the castle."

They explored the three main floors, popping doors open and shut, peeking around doorways, and examining paintings on the walls.

"Come on. Let's see where these stairs lead," Chris said. "It looks like some kind of tower."

They climbed up a winding stone staircase. When they got to the top, they both gasped. The view from the top was incredible. They could see beyond the far shore of Loch Ness, all the way to the distant mountains. They stood on a small walkway, high up on the tower, and gazed around. The wind was gusting, making it hard to talk.

"The view is really something," shouted Chris.

"You know it. I bet we can see fifty miles." Steve pulled out his camera and snapped a few pictures of the countryside.

"This wind is awesome!" yelled Chris, pointing down at the ruined fort on the shore of the loch. Then they saw Angus far below, walking into the stable. It was too hard to talk with the wind rushing around them, so they went back inside. They made their way down into the yard and headed to where they had seen the old man.

"Hi, Angus," they called. "How's it going?"

"Ah, lads," he answered. "Been having a look around?"

"Aye, that we have," said Steve, imitating Angus.

The old man laughed. "Been here only a day and already talking like one of us."

"Hey, Angus," said Chris as the old man began to brush a big, chestnut-colored horse. "Tell us some more about the ancient family treasure."

"Well," he answered, "there's not much more to tell. The old laird who they say buried the treasure was hanged by the English as a rebel, because he helped Bonnie Prince Charlie try to take back the throne. That was in 1746. If there ever was a treasure, he took the secret of where it was hidden to his grave. No trace of it was ever found."

"Have people tried to find it?" asked Chris.

"Sure, some have. But they didn't know

44

where to begin." Angus stretched out his arm toward the open fields and said, "The Highlands are mighty big. It would be easy to hide a treasure out there so no one could find it."

"Well, did he leave a map or anything—so he could find it later?" asked Chris.

"Or so somebody else could find it?" added Steve.

Angus thought for a moment. "Well, there's always been a silly legend about some kind of poem written by the condemned laird as he spent his last night on earth in his cell in Inverness."

"What?!?" shouted both boys at once. "A poem?"

"Aye, laddies. They say the old laird could look out the little window of the cell, between the iron bars, and he could see the gallows where he'd take his last look and his last breath. The legend says he wrote a poem as the rising sun shined through the window on his last morning. But for him, it was a setting sun."

Steve and Chris stared at each other, hardly believing what the old man had told them.

"Uh, listen, Angus," muttered Chris, "we've got to be going."

"Don't take this business about the poem

too seriously, lads. It's all just nonsense. And speaking of nonsense, have you had a chance to talk to Mary about a certain creature you were interested in?" Again, they noticed the twinkle in his eye.

"Uh, no, we haven't talked to her yet," Steve said. "But we definitely will. See you later."

"Unbelievable!" Chris said when the boys were back in their room. "Did you hear what Angus said? There's a poem that tells where the treasure is! This is great—I think we're really onto something." Chris was so excited he was pacing back and forth.

"It may not be just a legend after all," Steve said thoughtfully. "What we've got may be the poem that the condemned man wrote."

"But how did it get on the back of the picture? Who wrote it there?" Chris asked.

Steve said, "I don't know. But if the picture is really that old, a lot could have happened. Maybe the old laird told it to somebody before he was hanged and that person wrote it down."

"Yeah, maybe he whispered it to the hangman right before he slipped the noose around his neck. *For him, it was a setting sun,*" Chris added dramatically, imitating Angus.

Steve laughed. "Maybe it wasn't quite *that* dramatic. But somehow the poem got on the picture and now we know the poem."

"It's a good thing Fiona's got it now," said Chris softly. Looking around, he added, "I bet Duncan would give anything to get his hands on it."

"Yeah. We're going to have to be really careful. We don't know how much he knows. He always seems to be lurking around someplace. And he might get suspicious if he hears us asking people questions about the treasure."

"I get the feeling he's already suspicious," said Chris.

"Well, we'd better watch our step. He looks dangerous to me. And we have to take it slowly. We need to figure this thing out logically."

"You and your logic," Chris replied.

"Well, my logic tells me that it's time to eat something."

"Yeah, I'm hungry, too, now that you mention it. Let's see what we can find to eat," Chris said.

The boys bounded down the main stairs, two steps at a time. They found Mary, Angus's wife and the castle's cook, in the kitchen. Mary was a small, good-natured woman who looked about Angus's age. Her gray hair was tied back in a bun and her

47

cheeks were rosy from the heat of the big oven and stove.

The boys sat at the big work table while Mary fixed them some sandwiches. Because the group was out, she told them it seemed silly to set the table in the huge dining room for just two people.

The boys could tell she liked having company in the kitchen because she talked up a storm. All they had to do was listen. She explained to them how to make a haggis, a traditional Scottish food.

". . . then you chop up the sheep's heart and liver and lungs and put it all in the sheep's stomach bag with some oatmeal and onions, and boil it for a few hours. You have to prick the stomach with a fork every now and then or the haggis will explode. And we don't want that, do we, me lads?"

"Uh, no," answered Chris, looking a little green. "We sure don't want it to blow up."

"You weren't planning to serve this stuff to us, were you, Mary?" asked Steve, looking like it would be fine with him to skip the haggis for dinner.

Mary answered, with the same twinkle in her eye that they had seen in Angus's, "Oh, I don't know. I just might feel like making one."

"Great," muttered Chris so only Steve could

hear. "Boiled sheep guts in a sheep stomach. Maybe I'll just have a hamburger and fries."

Steve poked his cousin in the ribs. Then he cleared his throat and said, "Mary, Angus said that you've seen the Loch Ness monster."

Mary's face suddenly became serious. She stopped kneading the bread dough she was working with and wiped her hands on her apron.

"Aye," she said quietly, "I've seen something in the loch. I couldn't say if it was the monster everybody talks about or not. I just know that what I saw wasn't yer ordinary animal."

"Tell us about it, please Mary?" begged Chris.

Mary sat down and began her story.

"I was a teenager when it happened. I grew up on a farm about five miles from here and spent a lot of time as a girl in these parts, walking around the loch and such. One evening in April, I was walking alone on a bluff overlooking a part of the loch not far from here. The sun was going down, but there was still some light left. I was looking out over the loch and I saw something swimming about fifty feet offshore. At first I thought it was a large bird with its neck out of the water. But as I watched, it turned and swerved, and then

I knew it wasn't a bird. No bird is that big."

Chris and Steve sat still as statues, listening to every word. "What did it look like?" Chris asked in a hushed whisper.

"Its neck stuck out of the water a good eight or ten feet, and its head was flat, a little like a seal's head. I saw a hump in back, and it had what looked like flippers to help it paddle through the water."

"What did you do?" asked Chris.

"Well," she answered, "I had to sit down on a stone fence to catch my breath. Of course, I had heard the stories about a creature in the loch. But I never expected to see it, not in my wildest dreams. I had always thought of myself as pretty level-headed. But when I saw that creature swimming across the loch, I had the strangest feeling I'd ever had, or ever have had since."

"What was it?"

Mary paused for a moment. "It was like I was catching a glimpse of something special, something that people were never meant to see. I felt like I was lucky enough to peek through a curtain that no one else could peek behind."

Mary had a faraway look in her eyes, as if she were looking back across time, across space, through that secret curtain once again.

The boys were quiet. They didn't want to break the magic spell that the old woman had woven. But finally Steve asked, "Where exactly did you see it?"

It seemed like Mary had to tear herself away from the vision in her mind to come back to the present. "I was standing on the cliff out here, down by the old ruin. The creature was swimming out by what we call the Witches' Fire."

Steve and Chris's eyes met. It was hard to tell whose eyes were bigger at that moment. Steve silently mouthed the words, *Where witches burn.*

"Uh, what's that?" Chris managed to ask.

"It's a place out on the loch where, if the wind is blowing just right, the waves get whipped up and splash and dance around like dark flames. The people around here have called it that for hundreds of years because it looks like the terrible flames that danced around the witches when they were burned at the stake long ago."

Chris's mouth dropped open and Steve just stared at Mary.

"The Witches' Fire is a bad place," continued Mary. "I know other people who claim to have seen the creature out there. With that terrible name, it's a place with a curse on it, if you ask me. A terrible curse."

When Steve had recovered from his shock enough to speak, he asked in a hushed voice, half afraid to hear the answer, "Do you know anything about a star, a wolf, or a scar?"

Mary looked at him strangely and shook her head. "No laddie, I can't say I do." She seemed to shake herself out of her dreaminess and added, "I do know one thing, though. If I don't get started on this baking soon, there won't be any bread at dinner for all those hungry people when they get back! You lads run along now and let me get some work done."

As the boys stood up, they heard footsteps in the hallway leading to the kitchen. When they looked up they saw, standing in the door, the tall, dark figure of Duncan. He nodded a greeting to them and to Mary.

Chris and Steve slipped by the laird, yelling thanks to Mary for lunch, and heading for their room.

"Did he hear anything?" whispered Steve.

"I don't know," his cousin answered. "But it's almost like he's following us around. He always pops up. I know he's watching us. I just know it. We've got to be more careful."

Steve nodded grimly. "We can't afford to take any chances," he said.

Five

WHEN Chris and Steve slid into their seats at the long dining room table that night, they couldn't believe how talkative the group was. The six tourists were all talking at once about the sights they had seen that day. At first, no one heard Captain Ross clinking his spoon against his glass, signaling a toast. Paul helped out by clinking his spoon against his glass, too.

"Everyone, please. Captain Ross would like to speak," Paul said loudly.

The voices quieted down and Captain Ross stood up at the head of the table, his glass held high.

"A toast. To our fine American guests and our gracious hostess, Fiona Macgregor." As he tipped his glass toward the group and then toward Fiona, everyone applauded. Then the group began laughing and talking even more

53

loudly than before.

Chris and Steve enjoyed listening for awhile. But soon they grew restless. Steve rolled his eyes toward the outside. Chris knew what Steve was thinking.

"Dad, is it okay if we look around outside for awhile?" Chris asked. Paul was so busy talking that he didn't even hear Chris.

Steve stood up and walked over to where Paul was sitting. "Uncle Paul, Chris and I want to check out the outside of the castle for awhile. Is it okay?"

"What's that? Oh, sure, Steve. Have a good time," Paul answered absentmindedly.

As the boys went upstairs to get their jackets, Chris said, "Geez, I wish you had asked him for money. He's in a great mood!"

"I don't think he even heard what I said."

"It's probably better that way. He might not have let us go if he had really thought about it."

They stopped for a moment on the landing between the second and third floor.

"Did you notice that Duncan wasn't at dinner," Steve asked.

"Sure I noticed. I wonder if he just doesn't like to eat with the guests or if he was off somewhere?"

Just then, they saw Duncan staring down

at them from the top of the stairs. He stood stone-faced and unmoving.

"Uh, hi. We missed you at dinner," Steve said to the laird as he climbed his way up the rest of the steps.

Duncan answered slowly, "I had some unexpected business to attend to."

"Well, if you don't mind, we're going to explore outside the castle for awhile," Chris said, following Steve.

"Be careful. The night air can chill you to the bones here in the Highlands." Duncan then moved down the great stairway silently.

Chris and Steve reached the top of the stairs, ran down the hall, and shut the door to their room.

"I tell you, there's something really strange about that guy. I don't trust him," Chris said.

"I know what you mean. Maybe if we figure out the mystery of the poem, we'll be able to learn more about Duncan, too. Come on. Let's go."

They grabbed their jackets. "Hey, get my camera, will you?" asked Steve.

"Don't you ever get tired of lugging that thing around?" teased Chris. He handed it to Steve.

"Yeah," Steve answered. "It does get kind of heavy sometimes. Oh well, I guess it won't hurt to have it with us."

"Okay. But it's your shoulder that's going to get tired carrying it."

"I can handle it."

As they hurried down the steps, they could hear the voices of the guests coming from the sitting room.

Steve yanked open one of the double doors at the front of the castle. "This thing must weigh a ton."

"Now who's a wimp?" Chris asked, giving Steve a hand with the door.

"Where do you want to go first?" Steve asked when they were outside the castle.

"How about over there, across that field toward the loch?" Chris asked.

"Sounds like a good idea."

Even though the sun was about to set, it was still light enough to see. They walked in silence for awhile.

Chris finally broke the silence. "Have you noticed that the sun goes down a lot slower here than at home?"

"Yeah, it's because we're much farther north than Ohio. We're almost as far north as Juneau, Alaska."

"No kidding? You're a walking world atlas," Chris said as he walked ahead. Steve stopped to take a picture of the setting sun. He called out to Chris, "Look at this. What a shot!"

When Chris heard Steve and turned back to look, he tripped on a rock and fell to his knees. Suddenly, he found himself looking over a cliff that dropped about fifty feet down to the dark waters of Loch Ness. His hands were on the very edge of the dropoff. He could see the water lapping against the rocks far below. He shut his eyes, imagining a terrible sight—his crumpled body smashed on the rocks.

"That was pretty close," Steve said, running up to where Chris was. "Quit bugging me about being a walking atlas and watch where you're walking. Are you okay?"

"Y-yeah," answered Chris. "I'm okay." He stood up and brushed himself off. "Man, I hate to think what I'd look like if I'd fallen off this cliff." Chris stared over the edge.

"Hey," cried Steve. "Look back over there! It's the ruins of that old fort we saw from our bedroom window. Come on!"

The boys ran toward the ruin that overlooked the loch. When they reached the fort, they entered the grounds through a decaying gate. The tumbledown towers seemed much larger up close.

"This place must have really been something in its day. I wonder if there were any battles here?" Steve asked curiously. But

Chris was already on the other side of the ruined fort. He was examining a large hole in a wall facing the land side.

"Hey!" he yelled to Steve, "I think this was made by a cannonball. Come here and see."

When Steve didn't respond, Chris ran back and saw Steve staring thoughtfully up at the massive heap of ruined stone. Chris ran over to where his cousin was standing and asked, "What's on your mind?"

"You know what I'm thinking?" asked Steve. "I think this is the ruin in the monster picture."

Chris whistled. "Yeah, you're right," he said. "Here's the part that sticks up in the picture."

"And there's one of the windows. Oh man, this is too weird!"

They turned to gaze out over the loch. Chris pointed out over the water and said in a low voice, "If this is the ruin in the picture, then the monster would be somewhere right about there. And this must be the cliff in the picture," he added, sweeping his arm out to indicate the cliff he had almost fallen over.

Steve and Chris sat down on a wall that had partly fallen in. They stared in silence for a few minutes out over the calm surface of the loch, wondering what strange, unearthly secret its dark waters held. The wind was blowing stronger. They zipped their jackets.

"The way I see it," began Chris, "is that Duncan tried to steal the picture because he knew that it might lead to the treasure. He must have found out about the poem somehow and now he wants the treasure."

"And I think he's fighting with Fiona about something," added Steve. "They're always giving each other strange looks. I'm scared he might do something to her."

"Yeah, and if he knows that Fiona's got the picture with the poem, he might do anything to get it. I sure wouldn't want anything to happen to Fiona." Chris picked up a stone and tossed it over the wall.

Neither boy said anything for a time as they watched the sun slowly sinking. Then Steve broke the silence.

"You really like Fiona, don't you?"

"She's okay." After he was quiet for a time, Chris added, "You want to know something? You know how you've been teasing me about her maybe marrying Dad?"

"Hey, I was just fooling around."

"Yeah, I know. It's just that, well, I've been thinking a lot about it. You've got a mom who lives with you. I mean, Dad's a great guy and everything, and we have lots of fun together.

But sometimes I kind of wish I could have a mom, too—you know, a whole family. I know my mom and dad will never get back together again. When I was a little kid I used to think they might, but now I know better."

Chris looked out at the water and the hills beyond. Then he said in a quiet voice, "Fiona and Dad, well, they seem to really like each other. Sometimes I think it would be nice if, well, you know, maybe they could get married."

Steve jabbed Chris with his elbow. "You're not going to get all mushy on me, are you?"

Chris zipped his jacket up tighter around his neck and straightened up. "No way. It's just that I think we'd better tell Dad what we know. He can tell Fiona that she might be in danger from the laird. Maybe—"

"Shhh! Listen! What's that sound?" Steve asked sharply. "Do you hear it?"

They both listened, frozen in their places.

"I don't hear anything," whispered Chris. "Just the wind picking up. What was it?"

Steve shook his head. "You're not going to believe this," he said, "but it sounded like someone playing the bagpipes, way far away. It was like it came floating in on the wind and then disappeared."

"Oh, man, knock it off!" Chris snapped.

"You're just trying to scare me with that phantom bagpiper stuff!"

"No, honest, I really thought I heard something for a second," Steve said. "But maybe it was just a nighthawk or some other animal."

"Probably. But it's getting kind of scary out here," said Chris. "The sun's almost down."

"Yeah, maybe we better think about getting back to the castle," said Steve. "It's pretty late. It might be hard to see—"

He never finished. Because just then, Chris let out a terrible cry. He pointed out over the loch and tried to speak. But nothing came out except choking gasps. Finally he was able to blurt out, "W-w-what's that over there?!?!"

Steve squinted in the direction his cousin was pointing. Suddenly, he felt like his breath had been sucked right out of him.

Out near the place Mary had called the Witches' Fire was a long, dark shape, sticking out of the water in several places. There seemed to be a head on the front of the shape. It was moving across the dark waters of the loch, bobbing and swaying slightly from side to side.

"N-n-no! It c-c-can't be!" Steve said, sputtering. "It's g-got to be a bird or a fish or s-s-something!"

Both boys stared as the shape swam slowly

across the middle of Loch Ness. They felt paralyzed. Was it their imaginations playing tricks on them? Was it just a log or an animal? Or was it something else, something unnatural, something monstrous?

"Oh, my gosh!" shouted Chris, breaking the spell that held him prisoner. "The camera! Take a picture before it disappears!"

The words slapped Steve into action. He whipped his camera up to his face.

"Hurry!" Chris insisted. "Hurry!"

"I'm hurrying, I'm hurrying!"

After what seemed like an eternity, Chris heard the click of the shutter, once, then again. Then, before their eyes, the shape appeared to dive below the water. As quickly as it had appeared, it was gone.

"D-did you get it?" Chris asked, his voice trembling with excitement.

"Yeah, I think so. I don't know. The light wasn't very good. And my hands were shaking so much I don't know if it was in focus."

"Listen, whatever you do, be careful with that film! You might have the picture of the century!"

They gazed out at the Witches' Fire for several more minutes, hoping against hope that the creature would appear again. But it didn't.

"Man, oh, man. We must be in the twilight

zone. I can't believe it. I just can't believe it," Chris kept repeating. "You think you hear the bagpipes that are supposed to mean the monster is about to appear. And then we see that . . . that thing out there!"

They tried to calm down and get a hold of themselves as they walked slowly back across the field to the castle. The sun was gone now, and they had to step carefully along the rocky path in the darkness.

"The camera's okay?" asked Chris for about the tenth time.

"YES! I told you, I've got it right here. Stop worrying!"

"Don't trip and bust it," said Chris.

"Don't worry!"

When they got back to the castle, everything was quiet.

"It must be later than I thought," said Steve quietly, looking at his watch. "It's 10:30. Everyone's gone to bed."

"I'm sure they were all pretty beat after exploring all day. I'm going to find Dad and tell him what we saw."

"He's going to think you're crazy. He already thinks your imagination is out of control," Steve reminded Chris.

"Maybe I won't tell him yet. But I want to say good night so he won't worry about us."

They passed the silent drawing room. The dying coals in the huge fireplace cast strange and frightening shadows on the walls. The castle seemed friendly enough when its rooms were filled with laughing people. But now, when there was nothing in the dark rooms but an eerie silence and the shadows dancing wildly, the boys could feel the castle's secrets and hidden mysteries. They crept up the stairs, listening to the sounds of the centuries-old castle.

But when they came to the second floor landing and were about to climb to the third floor, they heard voices—angry, arguing voices. They were coming from behind a closed door near the staircase. Chris and Steve froze on the stairs in the darkness. They could barely hear the voices through the closed door.

"I'm doing what we have to do," said one voice. It was Fiona's. But her voice sounded hard and almost hateful—a tone they had never heard before.

"I never should have allowed it," said the other. The boys looked at each other. They recognized the voice of the laird of Castle Macgregor. They moved up the stairs and around the corner from the door to be able to hear better.

"It will be the ruin of the family," continued Duncan. "It is the darkest day in the long history of the Macgregors, worse than when our ancestor was hanged for his part in the Rebellion. And I blame you, Fiona Macgregor—no one else!"

Fiona didn't answer.

"I'm warning you," said Duncan, his voice rising. "Do not try to stop me. Do not stand in my way. Is that clear? Answer me!"

Still, Fiona said nothing. Finally, she answered in a low voice, filled with hate and anger, "I will not be ordered around by you. I will not!"

Suddenly, the boys heard the sound of quick footsteps. They shrunk back against the wall into the shadows. The closed door burst open and Fiona walked quickly down the dark hallway.

When her footsteps had died away, the door was slowly pulled shut. The click of the lock sounded as loud as a thunderbolt in the silent house.

Six

"CHRIS, wake up!"

"Huh?"

Chris struggled to open his eyes. He looked at the dial of his watch, glowing in the dark room. The moon must have already set, because it wasn't shining through the window. "What's wrong?" he muttered. "Another burglar?"

Steve sounded wide awake. "No, nothing like that," he said. "I can't sleep. I've been thinking about the poem."

Chris rolled over and switched on the light on his table. "You mean the poem on the back of the picture?" When Chris's eyes adjusted to the light, he saw that his cousin was holding the piece of paper with the poem written on it.

"Well, is it making any more sense at 2:30 in the morning than it does during the day?"

"I'm not sure," answered Steve slowly, "but I think I might have figured out something."

Chris suddenly felt wide awake. "What?" he asked anxiously.

"You know the first two lines of the poem?"

Chris repeated them from memory: *"Where witches burn, beware the Beast, When moon is full, look to the east."*

"Well," said Steve, "I think that means a person would have to go out to the Witches' Fire in a boat and then turn around and look back to the east. That would be toward that cliff we were near tonight, the one you almost fell off of when you tripped."

"Does it have to be when the moon is full? What difference would it make?"

"I don't know. But we're going to get the chance to find out."

"What do you mean?" asked Chris.

"I checked the calendar in my travel almanac. The night after next is the full moon."

Chris whistled softly. "You mean you want to go out on Loch Ness in a boat to the place where you and I and a lot of other people might have seen a monster? You're out of your mind!"

"I didn't say I wanted to go," Steve said. "In fact, it sounds pretty scary. But we don't have any choice if we want to find out if I'm right about the poem."

"But what do you think we'll see?"

"I don't know that either. Maybe we'll see

something when we look to the east that you can't see from any other place, only from the Witches' Fire. I don't know."

Chris was quiet for a long time. Then he said, "I guess maybe you're right. There's only one way to find out what we might see. But I'm not too excited about being out at the Witches' Fire in a little boat about the size of the Loch Ness monster's little finger."

"Neither am I," answered Steve.

"This trip is getting weirder and weirder." He reached over and switched off the light.

After a few minutes Chris said softly, "Steve, are you awake?"

"Yeah."

"I can't sleep. The monster and the poem, Fiona and Duncan fighting—all this stuff keeps zooming around in my brain," explained Chris.

"I know what you mean," said Steve.

Then after a pause, Chris asked, "Do you think that really was the creature we saw?"

"I don't know. Angus promised me he'd take the film into the village tomorrow to get it developed. Maybe the pictures will show something."

Somewhere far away in the foggy night, they heard the sound of bells chiming—three times. The sound was echoed a moment later by the ancient grandfather clock in the hallway two stories below.

"You know, it's one thing to see a monster from a cliff on shore," Chris said. "But now we're talking about going out on the loch in a dinky, little rowboat. If that thing really is a monster of some kind, well . . . , what I mean is . . . , we'll be sitting ducks."

"I know. I thought about that, too," Steve replied softly.

"Sitting ducks," repeated Chris. "For the Beast."

* * * * *

The next morning after breakfast, Steve gave Angus the film. Angus stuck the film in his jacket pocket, got into his car, and rolled the window down.

"Anything else you might be needing, laddie?" Angus asked.

"No, thanks. Just take good care of my film. I got some dynamite pictures of the sun setting."

"No need to fear. It's safe with me, lad," Angus replied. Then he rolled up the window, honked the horn, and drove off.

Steve watched Angus's little car crawl across the wide fields beneath the cloud-filled sky and disappear over a hill.

"Do you think the film will be safe with

Angus?" Chris asked as he walked up behind Steve.

Steve felt like he jumped about a foot high at the sound of Chris's voice.

"What's the idea, sneaking up on me like that?" Steve snapped.

"Hey, I'm sorry. I thought you heard me."

"Yeah, well, forget it. I guess I'm just kind of jumpy," Steve said apologetically.

"Let's go fill Dad in on what's been going on."

"Good idea," Steve agreed.

They found Paul in the dining room drinking coffee with Captain Ross.

"Uh, excuse us, Dad, but we have to talk to you for a second," Chris said. "It's important."

"Sure," Paul answered. "I'll catch you later, Jamie," he said to Captain Ross. "Let's try to leave in about forty-five minutes."

"Righto," said the captain.

Paul said, "Let's go up to my room, guys." The boys could feel Captain Ross watching them as they left the dining room.

They followed Paul upstairs to his room on the second floor. "Okay. What's up?" Paul asked, sitting down on the bed. Steve sat down on a chair, and Chris shut the door. Then they took turns explaining all about the poem, the legend of the lost treasure, and seeing the thing out on the loch.

70

"I don't know, guys," Paul said when they had finished. "It all sounds pretty far fetched. The poem is probably just some kind of verse, like Fiona said. And as for the monster—well, there have been lots of scientific studies and search expeditions. Nobody's ever found any proof—none at all."

Steve looked down. "I know it sounds weird, Uncle Paul," he said. "But the thing we saw on the loch didn't look like any ordinary animal."

"You said it was getting dark," said Paul. "Our eyes can play lots of tricks on us, especially when we've heard all the stories and legends."

"But what about the bagpipe Steve heard?" asked Chris.

"It was probably the wind or a bird, just like you said."

"Well, how about the treasure?" Steve asked.

"Look, you don't have any proof about anything," answered Paul. "I think it's just the atmosphere of this place. It makes you feel like almost anything could happen. Don't forget, that's why we came here in the first place—for the atmosphere."

"Don't you believe us, Dad?"

"I believe that you saw something on the loch that was probably a log or a duck or something," Paul said. "As for the poem and the treasure, who knows? The thing is, we don't have any way of knowing if it's all true or not. What more can I say?"

"But someone did try to break into our room," protested Steve.

"Yeah, but we don't know for sure what he was after," Paul replied. "He might even have broken into the wrong room." Paul leaned over and messed up Chris's hair affectionately. "If it was me, I'd go after that lawyer's video camera, not The Backpack from the Dumpster!" The boys laughed, but only a little.

"That's what I said," Steve added.

Just then the clock in the downstairs hall started to chime. They counted ten times.

"Shoot," said Paul. "It's 10:00 already. We've got to get going. Why don't you guys get your stuff together? We're going to Castle Kilmarnock today."

Chris and Steve looked at each other.

"Sure, okay," said Chris.

Ten minutes later, they piled into the van with the rest of the guests, Fiona, and Captain Ross.

"You'll really like this place, guys," Fiona said as Paul drove over the bumpy Highland roads. "Castle Kilmarnock has the biggest collection of armor and medieval weapons in northern Scotland."

The boys couldn't believe it! Castle Kilmarnock was even bigger than Castle Macgregor. Most of its rooms were used as a museum, but the family still lived in a small part of the castle. They had to open it up to paying visitors to make enough money to keep it.

"It's hard for some of the noble families here to open up their castles," Paul explained to the tour members as they waited in the great hall for the tour to begin. "But it's so expensive to keep these old places that they have to do it."

The tour lasted most of the morning and the group ate lunch in the huge dining room. After lunch the visitors were free to wander through the castle. Almost everyone went outside because the sun was shining for a change.

"Are you guys coming out?" Paul asked.

"In a few minutes, Dad," Chris said. "We want to look around inside a little more."

"I'm glad you kids came along. I've been kind of worried about you."

"We're okay, Dad. You worry too much."

Chris and Steve went back in the castle. Once inside, Steve said, "I've got something I want to show you. Follow me." Steve led him to a glass display case that held some maps and old pictures.

"Listen to this," Steve said, reading from a piece of paper in the case. "'Family treasure from this and other castles in this part of the Highlands were given to the laird of nearby Macgregor Castle for safekeeping from the English in 1746. After the period of confusion following the defeat of Bonnie Prince Charlie and the Rebellion, the collected treasure was never found. Its location has passed into the realm of fable and legend and may still be hidden somewhere in the barren moors and lonely fields around Loch Ness.' Wow, what do you think about that?"

"I think there might be a lot of treasure out there somewhere," said a voice from around the corner. The boys were startled, but turned around to see the smiling face of Captain Ross. He walked over to where they were standing.

"Some people have estimated that the trea-sure is worth over ten million pounds—that's over fifteen million dollars," explained the cap-tain. He laughed to himself and added, "Some people would probably do just about anything for that kind of money, wouldn't they?"

Chris caught Steve's eye before he answered, "Yeah, I guess so."

"Well, your father sent me down here to get you chaps. We're getting ready to leave."

Chris and Steve were pretty quiet on the ride back to Macgregor Castle. Chris knew that Steve was thinking about what they had seen and heard at Castle Kilmarnock. Chris was wishing that the full moon wasn't going to be so soon.

After dinner that evening, they joined the group around the fire in Castle Macgregor's great room. The room was so big that it made people's voices echo.

Paul and Fiona were having a great time singing old songs from their college days together. Captain Ross laughed at some of the lyrics and smoked his pipe. Only Duncan was missing.

"Sing 'Hey Jude' again, Paul!" cried the lawyer from San Diego, picking up his video camera. "I want to get some videos of you and Fiona singing together!"

"We could have used that guy's video camera yesterday when we saw that thing out on the loch," Steve whispered to Chris.

"You know it."

"I think I'm going to go to bed," said Steve, yawning. "Tomorrow night's the night."

"Yeah," answered Chris, standing up. "Full moon."

* * * * *

After breakfast the next morning, Chris waved to Angus as the old man was walking across the yard to the stables.

"Hey, Angus," said Chris. "Are there any rowboats around? We wanted to . . . explore the shoreline a little bit."

"Aye, laddie," the old man answered. "You'll find the boathouse down below the ruin. The boats are old, but they should keep out water long enough for you to look around the shore for a little while. But be careful. The loch can be dangerous when the weather is bad."

Chris went back inside. Steve was in their room studying a map of Loch Ness. Looking up, Steve said, "Your dad's about to leave for Inverness. He's taking the group there to buy souvenirs and go sightseeing."

"That means he'll be gone all day. Did he say anything about us not going?"

"Just that we should stay out of trouble."

"He always says that. Is Fiona going with them?" Chris asked.

"I don't know, why?"

"I just feel better when she's close to Dad. Duncan makes me nervous. You don't think he would hurt Fiona, do you?" Chris asked.

"I don't know. What do you think they

were arguing about the other night when we came in?"

"I don't know," Chris said. "But it didn't sound like they were discussing the weather—even though it looks pretty gray," he added, looking out the window. "If it doesn't clear up, we won't be able to see anything when the full moon rises."

They spent the morning in the castle, looking at dusty old books and maps that they found in the living room. Though they didn't see Duncan around anywhere, they could feel his presence. The door on the second floor that he had locked the night before last was still closed.

They ate lunch in the kitchen with Mary again, since they were the only ones around. "Have you worked for the laird for a long time, too, Mary?" asked Steve as they ate ham sandwiches.

"Oh, my, yes," she answered. "Not as long as Angus, you understand, but close to fifty years."

"So you must know Duncan pretty well," continued Steve.

"Oh, I wouldn't say that," Mary said with a smile. "No one knows the laird very well. He doesn't have many friends to my knowledge. He always keeps to himself."

"Yeah, we noticed," said Chris. "We hardly ever see him."

The boys smiled at each other when Mary sat down at the table. They had been trying to get her to talk about Duncan and it had worked.

"Laird Duncan Macgregor is an unusual man," said Mary. She looked around quickly as if she wanted to make sure no one was around. Even though the coast was clear, she lowered her voice.

"He's a very proud man," said Mary. "He's very proud of his family name and traditions. He loves the castle. I'd guess that he knows more about the Macgregor family and its history than anyone living."

"He's not very friendly," said Chris.

"Aye, he seems unfriendly to some people when they first meet him," explained Mary. "But I'd say he's reserved. He doesn't like to do things with people. And he won't go out of his way to be nice."

Mary stood up to check on something cooking in a big pot on the stove.

"That isn't that sheep guts and oatmeal stuff, is it, Mary?" asked Chris.

She laughed. "Don't worry now, laddie," she said. "I haven't made you a haggis—yet."

She sat back down at the table and leaned

over toward the boys. She looked around carefully and said, "I'll tell you a little secret, if you promise not to tell anyone."

Chris and Steve nodded and moved closer to Mary.

"Some people in the village are saying the laird has money problems. They think he might even have to sell the castle. That would practically be the death of Duncan Macgregor. He loves the castle so much that I don't think he would be able to live without it."

The pot on the stove started to boil over and Mary hopped up to lower the flame underneath it. When her back was turned, Steve whispered to Chris, "If Duncan needs money to keep the castle, that would explain why he's so anxious to get the treasure."

Chris nodded. Then he asked Mary when she returned, "Mary, do you know why Duncan and Fiona were arguing?"

Mary looked sad. "Ah, you've heard them, too, have you?" She shook her head. "It's only been for the past year or so that they've been like this. Everything used to be just fine. No one knows what it is, but we've heard them arguing, too."

Steve and Chris stood up and carried their dishes over to the big, old-fashioned sink. "I guess we'd better get going," said Steve.

"Thanks for lunch, Mary. It was great."

"Yeah," added Steve, "anything that isn't sheep lungs and heart is great with me!"

It had started to rain while the boys were talking to Mary in the kitchen. They spent the rest of the afternoon inside, waiting for Paul and the group to return from Inverness. When they finally heard the crunch of the van's tires on the gravel driveway outside, they went downstairs. They found Paul and the group taking off raincoats in the hallway.

"Hi, Uncle Paul," said Steve. "Have a good time?"

"Yeah, except for the rain," Paul answered. "I heard on the radio that's it's supposed to clear up tonight."

Chris caught his cousin's eye and nodded.

"We're going into the village to have dinner at the pub. Do you guys want to go?"

"No thanks, Dad. We're not hungry. Mary's been feeding us stuff in the kitchen all afternoon."

"Well, okay," answered Paul. "If you get hungry, ask Mary to get you something— maybe a haggis deluxe."

Steve groaned. Chris stuck his finger down his throat and pretended to gag.

"And do me a favor, guys. Be careful, okay? I don't want to have to worry about you."

Seven

"ARE you hungry?" asked Steve.

"Nah. Besides, I couldn't eat anyway. I'm too nervous."

Steve and Chris were sitting in big leather chairs in the library. Since Paul had left for the pub with Fiona, Captain Ross, and the group, it was very quiet in the castle. The only sound was the ticking of the grandfather clock in the hall.

"What time is it?" asked Steve.

"Almost eight." Chris got up and walked to the window. "It's stopped raining, just like Dad said."

Steve joined him at the window, gazing out at the red setting sun in the western sky. The boys looked at each other.

"It looks pretty clear out now," Steve said.

"I guess it's time to go," Chris murmured in a low voice.

"We can still back out of this, you know," Steve said softly.

Chris shook his head. "We've got to do it. This might be the clue we're looking for."

Steve took one last look out the window. He could see the dark surface of Loch Ness in the distance. "You're right," he said with a sigh. "I guess there's no other way."

Leaving the castle quietly, they made their way down to the boat house. There they found some old rowboats, just like Angus said they would. As the sun was setting, the boys put a pair of oars in what looked like the best boat and carried it to the shore.

"Are there any life jackets?" asked Steve. "We should have life jackets."

"No," said Chris.

"This boat looks like it hasn't been used for years. Do you think it's safe?" asked Steve nervously.

"I guess so. Besides, what are we going to do, swim out?" asked Chris.

Steve looked at the old rowboat. "Are you sure you want to go through with this?" he asked.

Chris took a deep breath. "Yeah. We have to find out if we can see anything, monster or no monster."

Both boys were silent for a moment, gazing

out over the dark surface of Loch Ness. It looked calm enough. But they were thinking about what terrible thing could be under the smooth surface of the loch.

"Let's go," said Chris, breaking the silence. "We've got maybe another hour before the moon rises."

They pushed out from the shore, Steve rowing and Chris holding the piece of paper with the poem on it. They had flipped a coin to see who would row first. Chris directed them toward the spot where they remembered the monster was shown on the old picture. Slender wisps of fog were rising off the surface of the loch.

It was slow going in the old rowboat, and Steve had trouble making it go where he wanted it to go. As the sun sank lower and lower in the sky, the shadows got longer and were black against the dark water. In the fading light, they heard the melancholy cries of a strange bird in the distance. They saw fish jump and disappear again into the depths of the loch.

After about thirty minutes, Chris said with irritation, "To the right. I think you're getting off course. Can't you keep this thing going straight?"

"I'm doing the best I can. It's hard to see."

"I know, I know. I'm sorry." Both boys were edgy and tense. And both kept looking around them at the dark water.

Suddenly Steve cried, "Chris! What's that over there?"

"Where?"

"That curvy thing sticking out of the water!"

They strained their eyes in the dusky light. Then Chris laughed. Steve breathed a sigh of relief.

"It's just a big branch," Steve said.

"Yeah," added Chris, laughing loudly to hide his nervousness. "The dreaded Loch Ness branch!"

After Steve rowed for about ten more minutes, Chris said, "I think the Witches' Fire should be right around here." Chris looked back toward the east, toward the cliff the ruin was on. "It's too dark," he said. "We can't see a thing."

"We have to wait until the moon rises. If there aren't any clouds covering it, there should be enough light to see."

"You know," said Chris after a while, "it's pretty peaceful out here. If we didn't know about the legends and everything, this could be really nice."

"Uh-huh," answered Steve. "If we didn't

know what we do know."

They talked a little about the treasure and about Fiona and Duncan. But soon they stopped talking, and each boy was alone with his thoughts. The minutes seemed like hours as they waited for the moon to rise. They listened to the waters gently lap against the side of their boat.

Finally, Steve said in a low voice, "Don't look now, but here it comes!" He pointed to the huge, reddish moon rising over the far shore of the loch.

"Boy," said Chris, "the moon looks huge when it's close to the horizon. And it's so orange. It's spooky."

"It'll get silvery when it gets up higher."

"What do you think we'll see, Steve? Do you think there's really a hidden meaning on the face of that cliff?"

"I don't know. But I hope we know what it is if we *do* see it."

It took another half an hour for the moon to rise high enough so it would shine on the face of the cliff. The boys stared at the cliff, trying hard to look for something, anything, that would reveal the poem's mysterious secret.

The cliff face was thrown into odd patterns of light and shadow by the moonlight. Rocks, ledges, and small trees jutted out from its surface. Shapes appeared, then vanished, as clouds covered the moon.

"Say the poem again, Chris," said Steve after they had gazed at the cliff for several minutes without talking. "Maybe it'll help us look."

Chris said in a low voice, "'Where witches burn, beware the Beast, when moon is full, look to the east. Above the wolf, below the star, turn blood to gold, rip open the scar.'"

"I don't know—all this stuff about blood and scars and wolves," said Steve. "It's hopeless! We're just looking at a dumb rock cliff! I was stupid to think we could figure it out. Your dad was right. It *is* just a verse of some kind or something." He slammed his fist against the side of the boat.

"Take it easy," said Chris. "What about the Witches' Fire and the Beast? We already know *that* means something. Don't give up yet. The moon is still rising. Maybe it has to be all the way up in the sky or something."

Steve didn't answer. He just put his chin on his hand and stared at the cliff. Neither boy spoke as the moon rose higher and higher in the night sky. Thousands of stars came out and then disappeared behind clouds. Staring up at the wide sky, the boys had never felt so tiny and helpless, or so alone.

They both saw it at the same time.

"Look!" screamed Steve. "That long, dark shape running down the middle of the cliff!"

"I see it! It looks . . . like . . . like a scar!"

"It must be some rock jutting out that casts a shadow when the moonlight hits it just right," said Steve.

"And look there, below it. There's water dripping down!" screamed Chris. "It must be a stream running down the cliff face."

"With the moonlight shining on it," said Steve, "it looks like . . . dripping blood!"

"It's the scar! It's the scar!" shouted Chris. He stood up in the boat, causing it to rock dangerously from side to side.

"Hey, have a seat," Steve said, pulling his cousin down. "Unless you want to take a bath."

Chris sat down again and the boys exchanged high fives. Before their astonished eyes, the rays of moonlight hit full on the cliff face. As the angle of the rays changed, the shadows changed shape. About halfway up the dark scar, a patch of darkness that had been just a shapeless blob was transformed into the shape of a star!

Both boys stared in disbelief. The meaning of the poem was becoming clear before their eyes, transformed by the magical power of the full moon! But their wonder soon turned to something very close to terror.

"There! A little ways up from the bottom of the scar," said Chris in a trembling voice. "That's the shape of . . . of . . . a wolf's head!"

"Oh, no!" cried Steve. "I don't believe it!"

"What?"

"I forgot my camera! It's lying on my bed," Steve answered. "In all the excitement, I just forgot about it!"

"Well, try to draw a map of the cliff face. Show the scar and the other shapes. Quick, before the shadows disappear."

Steve pulled a pen from his jacket pocket and sketched the cliff face on the back of the paper with the poem on it. He drew in the scar, the star, and the wolf's head. "There's just enough light," he said. When he was done he held out the drawing to Chris.

"Way to go, Picasso," Chris said. "That should be good enough to show where the places are, even during the day, when you can't see the shadows."

"It must mean that the treasure is buried along that thing that looks like a scar, between the wolf and star shapes," said Steve. "Rip open the scar—that means dig there!"

"Yeah. It's really a great place to hide

something. Whoever put it there knew that it would be almost impossible to find. You can't see the scar and other shapes from the cliff above. And people would be afraid to come out on the loch, especially out here to the Witches' Fire," said Chris.

"You know what, Chris?" asked Steve in a low voice, filled with fear. "I think what we know now could be very dangerous. I think certain people might be willing to do something terrible to us if they thought that we had solved the riddle of the treasure. We've got to protect this information."

Chris nodded in the moonlight. "Duncan," he said. "We have to keep him from finding out about this. Who knows what he'd do if he found out?"

As the minutes passed, they watched as the moon clouded over and the shapes seemed to melt away. It was hard to believe that just a few minutes before, when the moonlight was just right, they had been able to read the hidden meaning of the poem on the cliff face. Now, as if magically erased by a powerful, unseen hand, all the clues had vanished into thin air, leaving only a rocky cliff face—the perfect hiding place.

They waited a little while longer until they decided they had better return to shore. The wind seemed to be picking up again and the stars were completely hidden by clouds. A thick fog was settling in over the loch.

"Come on," said Steve. "Let's get back. It looks like a storm's coming up. We don't want to get caught out here in this dinky, little boat."

"Right," answered Chris, "Let's switch places, it's my turn to—hey! Steve! My shoes are soaked. The boat must be leaking!"

"Oh no! There's a big pool of water here in the back!" said Steve, feeling the bottom of the boat. "We've got to hurry!"

Chris jumped up and joined Steve at the oars. Sitting side by side, they rowed hard, trying not to panic. The fog had grown thicker, so thick that they couldn't see the shore anymore.

"It's harder to row now that the boat's got water in it," Chris yelled. "Harder!"

Together they pulled on the oars, racing desperately against the growing pool of water in the bottom of the boat. It had grown to cover the whole bottom up to about two inches. They felt the coldness on their ankles as the water sloshed from front to back.

"The faster we row, the faster the water comes in!" said Chris. "But we can't stop, we've got to go faster!"

After they had been rowing for what seemed like hours, Steve gasped, "I don't know how much more I can go." He was gulping for breath and moaning with each hard pull on the oar. Their muscles were stinging like someone was sticking sharp needles right into their bones. They knew that when the water level inside the boat reached the upper edge of the side, the small rowboat would sink like a stone and disappear below the dark water—with them in it.

"We've got to keep going!" cried Chris as he sucked air into his burning lungs. "We must be getting closer—unless we're off course."

"I can't see a thing. What if we're going in the wrong direction? And my arms feel like they're going to fall off," Steve moaned. "It's no use!"

"Come on, come on, we can do it," repeated Chris over and over as they moved slowly through the darkness.

"The water's almost up to my knees!" Steve said with a terrible groan. "I can't go on! We'll never make it! We're going to drown out here!"

Eight

J UST as Steve spoke, the bottom of the boat scraped against some rocks. Then it skidded to a stop on the sandy shore. They didn't know how long they lay there exhausted on the shoreline. When they finally recovered from their near escape, they dragged themselves to their feet.

"Have you still got the drawing of the shapes on the cliff?" Chris asked.

Steve felt in his shirt pocket and nodded. "Yeah. It's pretty dry."

"Think you can run?" asked Chris.

"Yeah, I think so," answered Steve. "As long as I don't have to use my arms."

"Let's go!"

Fat raindrops started to fall on them halfway up the path to the castle. The thunder and lightning began just as they reached the shelter of the front hall. They closed the heavy oak doors behind them and took off their soaking jackets.

"We have to tell Dad right away," whispered Chris. "He'll know what to do."

Chris and Steve stood in the hallway at the door to the drawing room. Paul was pacing nervously in front of the fireplace. Fiona sat on a sofa nearby, her face glowing in the firelight. Paul noticed them after a few minutes. Chris motioned for him to come out in the hall. They watched as Paul said something to Fiona and stood up. He came over to them.

"Where have you two been? I was afraid that. . . . What happened to you guys?" he asked. "You look like a couple of drowned rats!"

Steve glanced at Chris and answered, "Uh, we sort of got caught in the storm."

"Dad, we have to talk to you again—alone," said Chris. "It's really important."

"Why don't you get dry first," said Paul. "You don't want to catch a cold. Come on into the drawing room and stand in front of the fire."

"This can't wait, Dad."

Paul looked carefully at his son's serious face. "Fair enough," Paul said. "Let's go someplace where we can talk."

After grabbing two coats from the coatrack in the hall, he led them to a small, dark room off the main hallway near the staircase. The walls were lined with bookcases housing old, leather-bound books. A desk and chair were in one corner of the room. Several big armchairs faced the window and another sat beneath a large painting of some eighteenth-century Macgregor, who stared unsmilingly down at them.

"Let's go in here," said Paul. "This is some kind of study or something. I don't think anyone uses it."

He draped the coats over the boys' shoulders, and they sat down on some chairs near the window. The only light came from the lightning outside.

"That's the Macgregor who was hanged in 1746," said Paul, pointing to the picture on the wall across the room. "The one the legend says hid the treasure and wrote the poem."

The boys gazed at the painting, which seemed to stare back at them. The cruel eyes, hard mouth, and the dark hair were familiar. The old laird in the painting looked very much like Duncan.

Forcing themselves to look away from the haunting portrait, Steve and Chris sat down in chairs across from Paul and told him all about what they had learned out on the loch.

Paul frowned as he listened to the boys tell

their story. When they had finished, he said, "First of all, I have to tell you how angry I am that you two would do something so stupid. What if something had happened to you out there? No one even knew where you two were."

The boys both looked down at their feet—avoiding Paul's eyes. They knew Paul was right.

"From now on," Paul continued, "I want you to check in with me before you go wandering off. Is that understood?"

Chris and Steve nodded in agreement.

"I'll tell you boys, I thought your imaginations were running wild earlier, but now it sounds like you've really stumbled onto something. It's incredible. At first I thought the poem was just some crazy old legend or joke. But now I see it's more than that—a whole lot more."

"You have to tell Fiona, Dad. She might be in danger. She's got the poem and the picture, and Duncan might want to get them. He could be looking for the treasure, too, especially since Mary says he has money problems." Steve gave Chris a pointed look. Chris sighed. "Oh darn, we weren't supposed to tell that to anyone."

"And you know the looks he gives her,"

added Steve. "I don't think they're very good friends. I'm worried he could do something horrible to her."

"When we were at school together, she used to tell me that she always looked up to him, admired him," said Paul thoughtfully. "But something's gone wrong. Something's happened since those days."

"You have to warn her, Dad. You *have* to explain to her about where the treasure is so she can get to it before Duncan does," Chris pleaded.

Paul scratched his beard as he thought for a moment. Then he said, "Okay. I'll tell her everything and let her decide what to do."

A flash of lightning was followed by a tremendous peal of thunder. Paul and the boys heard the sound of a book dropping behind them. Looking over, they saw a figure underneath the large painting on the wall. Then another flash of lightning lit up the room.

There, beneath the painting of his ancestor, stood the grim-faced laird of Castle Macgregor. His steely eyes reflected the flash of the lightning and his voice was cold as he said, "Excuse me. I was just getting a book I needed. I didn't know anyone was in here." As the thunder boomed and rolled away, Duncan walked silently from the room. He left so quickly that the boys wondered if they had really seen him in the room. All that was left was the gloomy painting of Duncan's ancestor, staring down at them with the same cruel eyes.

"How long was he standing there?" whispered Steve.

"I don't know," answered Paul. "I didn't hear him come in."

"You've got to go to Fiona now, Dad—and fast," Chris pleaded. "If Duncan did overhear everything, we don't have much time."

"Fiona doesn't have much time," added Steve.

* * * * * *

The next day was drizzly and cloudy. Whenever it looked like the sun was about to break through, black clouds would gather and the rain would start again.

Paul checked in on them. "Hey, boys. We're off to see some old churches this morning. Why don't you come along so I don't have to worry about you?"

Chris sneezed. "Gee, Dad, I'd like to, but I've got this cold."

Paul walked over to Chris and felt his head. "It feels like you might have a slight fever. Why don't you just stay in bed? I'll have

Mary bring some tea up to you. Anyway, I have to go, I have some last-minute details to get organized before we tour the churches. What about you, Steve, do you want to join us?"

"No, thanks, Uncle Paul. I have a headache."

"By the way, I spoke to Fiona," Paul said. "I told her everything—about the poem, the shapes on the cliff face, and your suspicions about Duncan."

"What did she say?" Chris asked.

"She was glad you wanted to tell her and she asked me if I'd tell you guys that you did the right thing. She also said that you have both become very special to her."

Steve couldn't tell if Chris was blushing when he heard this or if he was just feverish.

"Well," said Steve, "that's a relief, now that she knows about everything."

"Yeah," added Chris, "now she can be careful."

Paul left with the group and the boys spent the gloomy day in their room, staring out the window at the gray skies and trying to come up with some sort of plan.

"We've got to find a way to the treasure," Steve said.

"I think we could get together enough ropes

and stuff to try climbing the cliff face," Chris suggested.

"I don't know," said Steve. "The cliff here is really a lot bigger than the ones we've climbed on back home. And the weather's bad. Besides, we couldn't do it without telling your dad. He'd kill us if we tried something as dangerous as that without telling him."

"You're right. Maybe we can talk him into helping us climb down the cliff. He's a great rock climber. Let's ask him when he gets back."

At dinner that night, Chris and Steve could feel tension in the air. Even the tour group could sense that something was wrong. Paul was nervous. He tried to entertain the guests by telling lots of funny stories about other trips he had led. The group seemed to enjoy them.

But the thing that worried the boys most was that Fiona, Captain Ross, and Duncan were all missing from dinner. All Mary had said was that Duncan told her he wouldn't be at dinner. That wasn't unusual. But Fiona and Captain Ross had always been there.

After dinner, the boys drew Paul aside and asked him about getting some ropes and climbing down the cliff face to look for the treasure.

"Absolutely not!" Paul said firmly. "I've got the tour group, so I'm too busy to help. And anyway, it's way too dangerous. That cliff looks really treacherous. This is a matter for the police. They're the ones who should decide what to do. And I'm taking the van into Inverness right after dinner to talk to the police."

"What do you think they'll say?" asked Steve.

"I don't know, but I think it's a good idea to let them know what's going on. I'm worried about Fiona. No one seems to know where she is. I think the tour group suspects something's going on, but I don't want them to worry about anything. They'll just be staying around the castle tonight."

Paul's voice became very serious. "Now listen carefully. While I'm gone, I want you to stay in your room with the door locked. That way, if Duncan did overhear everything that we talked about and does decide to try anything, you'll be okay. Do you understand? Don't leave your room."

"What do you think he might try?" asked Steve.

"Who knows?" answered Paul. "But we don't want to take any chances."

Chris remembered the cruel, hard look in

Duncan's eyes when he surprised them in the study. He shivered, but not from the cold. "Sure, Dad, we understand," he answered.

Paul put his hand on Chris's shoulders. "Good. I know I can count on you guys. And I think Fiona knows she can count on you, too."

They followed Paul to the front hall and watched as he put on his coat. "Now remember," Paul said. "Stay in your room and be careful. I'll be gone for a few hours. I'll see you as soon as I get back."

"Don't worry, Dad. We'll be careful."

They watched the red taillights of the van disappear through the gate in the wall. Chris and Steve looked at each other.

"Let's go upstairs," said Steve. "There's nothing we can do. We'll just have to wait."

Time passed slowly up in their room. Mary brought tea and some homemade Scottish shortbread. Chris and Steve played cards.

"Come on," said Steve after they had played several hands. "That was a really stupid move. You're not concentrating on the game."

Chris stood up. "I know I'm not. I guess I'm worried—about everything. We still don't know where Fiona is," he said as he walked over to look out the window. "I have a feeling that something bad is happening to her—something that has to do with Duncan."

"It's a bad sign that he's missing, too," added Steve. "Hey, you've got to do something to take your mind off of it until your dad gets home. We can't do anything until then."

Chris sneezed. "I guess you're right." He sat back down at the table. "Pass me a tissue, will you? Okay, I'll try to concentrate. Let's start over."

They played for about half an hour, and Chris was actually winning the game. Steve looked at the cards in his hand with a worried look on his face. "Let's see, what am I going to—"

Just then they heard a soft, scratching sound, followed by fast footsteps in the hallway. Both boys looked up.

"What was that?" asked Chris.

"Oh, it's probably just somebody in the tour group going to bed," said Steve. "I'll check." He stood up and walked to the door. "Hey! What's this?" he cried, looking at the floor by the locked door.

Chris sprang up and ran to his cousin's side.

"It's an envelope!" said Steve. "Somebody slipped it under the door."

Chris fumbled with the old lock on the bedroom door. "This stupid thing! It's stuck! I can't get it open!" he shouted.

They fiddled with the lock for several minutes until they were finally able to work it. "Great!" said Chris angrily. "Whoever put this under the door is probably halfway to Inverness by now!"

They opened the door and Chris looked up and down the hall. There was no sign of anyone. He came back into the room.

"It's addressed to us," said Steve. "I don't get it!"

He ripped open the envelope and unfolded the piece of paper inside. Together the boys read:

Steve and Chris,
Please come to the old stone ruin on the cliff above the loch as soon as you can. Bring the drawing of the shapes on the cliff. I need your help desperately.

Fiona

Nine

S TEVE and Chris stared at the note.

"It's definitely Fiona's writing," Chris said.

"How do you know?" Steve asked.

"When Dad got that welcome letter from Fiona, I remember checking out the envelope because it was from Scotland. Then I noticed that Fiona's writing had these little curlicues on certain letters. Do you see what I mean?" Chris asked as he showed the note to Steve.

"And you tell me I'm the smart one," Steve said. "So what do you think we should do?" he asked anxiously.

"I-I don't know," his cousin answered, sitting down on the bed. "We promised Dad we'd stay here. But Fiona must be in big trouble, or else she wouldn't write to us like this."

"Now, wait a minute. This doesn't make sense. If Fiona's in trouble, then who slipped this note under the door?" Steve asked.

"I don't know," Chris said, blowing his nose.

"I think it must be some kind of trick or something," Steve said.

"But why would Fiona trick us?" Chris asked.

"I don't think she would. But someone else might."

"Someone like Duncan," Chris said.

"Right."

"But even if it is a trick, Fiona may still need us," Chris said with concern.

"For sure. And one of the last things your dad said before he left was that Fiona knows she can count on us."

"Yeah, but what do we do? Do we keep our promise to Dad or do we go help Fiona?"

"I don't know. What would your dad want us to do?" asked Steve.

Chris was silent for a minute. Then his eyes met Steve's. "I think, knowing the way he feels about Fiona," said Chris slowly, "that he would want us to help her. I mean, he's not here. Who else could she turn to except us? We can't let her down. It would be like letting Dad down, wouldn't it?"

Steve stood up and walked around the room without answering. Finally, he nodded in agreement. "Yeah, I guess you're right. I hate to disobey your dad. But what else can we do? We're the only ones who can help Fiona—

whatever kind of trouble she's in."

"Okay, then. Let's go. Is it still raining?"

Steve looked out the window at the sky. "No, I think it stopped. But it's getting pretty foggy."

They put on their jackets and grabbed a flashlight.

"Here. You better take some of these,"

Steve said as he handed Chris a bunch of tissues.

"Thanks," Chris said, stuffing the tissues in his pocket.

"I've got the map of the cliff side," Steve said as they walked out of the room and pulled the door shut behind them.

Steve and Chris went quietly down the stairs and slipped out the front door. The front yard of the castle was deserted.

They didn't speak until they were outside the castle gate. The air had turned cold and a chilling breeze was blowing. Clouds blew across the moon, making eerie shadows and shapes on the fields. When the moon was covered by the clouds, it got so dark that they needed the flashlight to see the path.

Out on the moor heading toward the loch, the fog was getting thicker. They had to stick close together or else they would lose each other.

"It's really weird walking through this fog," said Steve. "Sometimes I can barely see my hand in front of my face."

"Yeah, you know it," answered his cousin between sneezes. "I'm getting a case of the creeps."

When they had been walking in silence for about ten minutes, they were startled by a weird croaking that sounded like it came from right beside them.

"Aaahh!" cried Chris, jumping aside. "What's that?"

Then they heard the flapping of wings. In the darkness they could just make out the black shape of a large bird flying off.

"It's a raven," whispered Steve. "Mary told me that some people think they're the souls of dead people trying to find rest."

"Geez," muttered Chris.

After a few more minutes of careful walking, Chris froze and said, "Shh! Did you hear that?"

"Yeah. It sounded like a twig snapping or something."

Suddenly, a hare burst out of the underbrush on the side of the path they were following. They saw its white tail bobbing in the moonlight. The boys breathed more easily after they saw the hare running off.

"Whew," said Chris. "I guess I'm pretty jumpy."

"Yeah," answered Steve. "I know what you mean. It's just about as creepy out here as it can get."

They walked along without talking for the rest of the way to the old fort.

Chris sneezed, then blew his nose. "I don't know. Do you think we're lost? It seems like we should have been there by now."

"If we don't find the ruin pretty soon, I think we should go back. You sound sick, and if you want to know the truth, I'm getting scared."

Just then, they saw the fort through a break in the fog. There it stood—its dark shape looming on the edge of the cliff, with the waters of Loch Ness far below. Chris and Steve stopped about thirty feet from the fort.

"Turn off the flashlight," said Chris in a low voice. "We don't know who's in there. We don't want them to know we're coming until we know it's safe."

Chris pointed through a hole in the ruined wall where a window used to be. There, in the yellow light of a single lantern, was Fiona. She was walking back and forth in front of the lantern, wringing her hands and looking around.

"She looks really nervous," whispered Steve.

"Or scared. Come on."

With Chris leading the way, the boys walked over the rocky path up to a hole in the fort wall. Stepping as carefully as they could over the rock and rubble, they crept up to look in the window.

"I think she's alone," Chris whispered into Steve's ear. Steve nodded.

"Fiona!" said Chris in a low voice, trying not to surprise her. "It's us, Steve and Chris."

Fiona jumped and looked around. "Steve! Chris! In here!" she called back. Her voice sounded desperate.

They followed the sound of her voice around through a narrow passage. Ahead in a larger room they saw the yellow glow of the lantern.

When the boys reached the large room, they saw that it was open to the sky. Standing in the middle, surrounded by large chunks of rock that must have fallen from the walls, was Fiona.

"We came as fast as we could!" said Steve, as he and Chris rushed up to her.

"I've got the map of the cliff face," said Chris.

"Good," she answered. Her voice sounded strange and cool, not like it had ever sounded before. "I'm very glad to see you."

"So am I," came a voice from behind a large rock.

The boys turned to see Captain Ross walking toward them from out of the shadows. He had a strange smile on his face. And he was pointing a gun straight at them!

Ten

N OW, if you lads will just step over here," said Captain Ross, "I'll tie you up nice and neat with this rope." He motioned with the gun for Chris and Steve to stand facing the wall.

"Fiona!" cried Chris. "W-w-what's going on? Don't let him do this!"

But Fiona said nothing. She just looked away.

"Hey!" said Steve, his voice thick with growing fear. "Y-you can't do this. This is a joke, right?"

Captain Ross snickered. "This is no joke, laddie. I assure you."

The boys stared at him. Could this be the same man who had been friendly and jolly during the whole trip? They saw the evil smile and burning look in his eyes. It was the look of a wild beast that had its prey within its grasp.

Ross tightened the ropes on Steve's hands

with a hard jerk. The boy cried out in pain.

"Leave him alone!" yelled Chris.

Ross turned to stare hard at Chris. The man's eyes were wild in the flickering lantern light. He began to raise his hand as if to hit Chris, but Fiona held his arm.

"No, Jamie," she said softly.

Ross looked at Fiona for a second, then lowered his arm. The unnatural, frozen smile returned to his cruel face.

"I can understand why you're upset, lad. I apologize. I see now that I owe you boys an explanation." His voice was cool and dry again, without the slightest hint of emotion. It made the boys' blood run cold.

Ross finished tying Chris's hands. "Have a seat," he ordered, pushing the boys onto the wet, rocky ground. Fiona started forward, but a harsh look from Ross froze her where she stood.

"First of all," began Ross as he slipped the pistol into his coat pocket, "I want to thank you for doing all the hard work for me . . . for us." He looked at Fiona.

"I've been fascinated by the lost treasure of the Macgregors ever since I was a boy growing up on a dirt-poor little farm on the other side of the loch. I first discovered that there might really be a poem when I was working in the library in Inverness. I spent years and years researching, looking through old papers, books, maps, and journals. Sometimes I would think I was close to finding the key to the secret, then it would disappear. Finding out that I had gone down yet another blind alley almost drove me insane with anger and disappointment. But then one night, looking through an old diary, I learned about the etching and that the poem and the treasure really did exist."

Chris and Steve stared at the captain.

"So, Fiona and I became friends," continued the captain, putting his arm around Fiona. "In fact, we're secretly engaged."

Chris gasped. "N-n-no," he muttered. "I don't believe it!"

Ross nodded. "Oh, yes. But it's a secret engagement. Don't tell anyone," he added with a sickening laugh. "I learned from Fiona that she had given the etching to your father many years ago. I knew that the poem was on the back of that picture, so I had her get it back. You took very good care of it. We were a little afraid that Duncan would find out that you had the etching. So I tried to take it off your hands the first night you were here."

"You!" cried Steve. "You were the burglar in our room!"

Ross smiled again. "Unfortunately, I wasn't a very good thief. But you gave it to Fiona

112

first thing the next morning when the laird wasn't around. So he didn't find out that we had it. Everything worked out just fine."

"B-but we thought Duncan was the robber," said Steve. "We thought he was after the poem and the treasure."

Ross laughed again. "Old Duncan's a lot of things, but he's not a thief."

Fiona, who had been quiet the whole time Ross was talking, said, "The map, Jamie."

Ross smiled again and said to the boys, "Ah, yes. I wonder if I might trouble you for that map that you were so clever to draw— and let Fiona know all about. I think we have your delightful father to thank for that."

"You shut up about my father!" yelled Chris. "If he were here right now, you wouldn't be acting so cool!"

Ross's eyes glowed evilly in the foggy light. He kneeled down and snarled in Chris's face, "Watch what you say, you little wildcat. If your cousin and you had a horrible accident out here, no one would ever know, would they?"

Chris let out a little whimper of fear. Steve's body started trembling uncontrollably.

"The smart-alecky one has a temper, doesn't he?" Ross said to Fiona.

"Just get the map," she said. "Don't pick on them."

"The map," Ross ordered. "You can either tell me where it is, or I'll find it myself. And if I have to find it myself, I won't be very gentle."

The boys' eyes met. Steve nodded. "B-better give it to him. We don't have any choice," he said.

"It's in my coat pocket," muttered Chris, his head down.

Ross grabbed Chris's hair and jerked his head up. "What? Speak up, I didn't hear you!"

"It's in my pocket!" shouted Chris.

The captain reached into Chris's pocket and snatched out the paper with the map on it. Like a wolf devouring some dead animal, he studied it quickly in the light of the lantern. He showed it to Fiona, who nodded.

"All right," she said to Ross. "Let's go, now that we've got what we want. We've put the boys through enough."

Then Ross's face turned toward the boys. The smile on his face looked absolutely devilish. His fiendish eyes looked as if they were no longer the eyes of a human being.

He turned to Fiona. "Ah, I'm sorry, my dear, but there is one more thing," he said quietly. "I'm afraid we haven't, as you said, put the boys through quite enough."

For the first time, Fiona looked confused. "I-I don't understand, Jamie."

Ross patted the map against his head, as if he had forgotten something. "Here's how it is, dear," he explained. "The sad fact is that the boys know too much. How could you possibly think that we could let them go, knowing what they know about us? How very silly of you to think that, darling."

She stared at Ross. "W-what do you mean?"

"Don't be stupid, Fiona. I mean that the lads are going to go climbing on the cliff face. I've already put some ropes out there. But unfortunately, they're going to have a little accident, a nasty fall that I'm afraid they won't survive."

"Noooo!" shrieked Steve and Chris.

"Scream all you want," said Ross. "No one can hear you. No one will ever hear you."

"No, Jamie," cried Fiona, throwing herself at Ross. "You said you wouldn't hurt them! You promised you wouldn't!"

The captain pushed Fiona away roughly. "Things have changed, my dear. They've led us right to the lost treasure—their dead bodies are worth five million pounds apiece to us. Or to me, if you're not interested anymore. Are you changing your mind?"

Fiona began to cry and hit the captain with her fists. "No! You tricked me! How could you do this?!?!"

"Shut up!" Ross shoved Fiona to the ground.

As she fell, she hit her head against a rock. Fiona moaned and lay still.

"Good," Ross said sharply. "Now she won't bother me." Turning to Chris and Steve, he ordered, "Come on, you little brats, get up. It's time for your climb—and your swim afterward!"

He took out his revolver and grabbed Steve by the coat. He dragged him to his feet and then did the same to Chris. "Get going—walk!"

Steve's knees buckled under him and he fell to the ground. Ross kicked him in the side. Steve howled in pain like a hurt animal. "Get up! Quit stalling!"

Grabbing the lantern off the table, Ross poked Chris in the back with the revolver and forced both of them down the passageway out into the open. The fog was so thick that the moon and stars were completely invisible. Ross looked up into the sky and said, "Not a very nice night, is it, lads? Your father's going to think you were very foolish to go climbing on the cliff on a night like this."

"Please don't kill us!" cried Steve hysterically. "We won't tell anyone. We promise we won't. We don't care about the money."

Captain Ross only laughed.

"You'll never get away with this!" said Chris. "They'll catch you!"

"You couldn't be more wrong, lad. They

won't find out in a hundred years. And that's just about enough time to spend that ten million pounds!"

With Ross poking and pushing them, the boys finally reached the edge of the cliff. On the ground were some ropes arranged to look like they were used to climb the cliff. The boys stared at the ropes, speechless with fear.

"I've done a bit of climbing myself," said Ross, "when I was in the army. The knots are all tied perfectly. Except for one small mistake in one knot that's going to slip and come loose. It's a mistake anyone could make, especially a pair of young climbers like yourselves."

"No, please," whimpered Chris. "No."

"Shut up!" Ross yelled. Then more quietly, he explained, "I'm going to cut your ropes one by one with this knife and then just give you a little shove over the edge. I'll throw the ropes over after you. And then somebody will find you, washed up on the shore. Good-bye, lads. It's been a pleasure working with you to find the treasure." He laughed his fiendish laugh.

He cut the ropes that bound Chris's hands and grabbed him roughly from behind, pinning his arms at his side. The iron grip around his neck choked Chris. Chris squirmed and pulled, but his struggles were useless. Ross's strength was like a madman's.

Chris felt the barrel of the revolver digging into his back. Steve watched helplessly, knowing he was next.

Ross wrestled him to the very edge of the cliff and said, "Have a nice swim."

Chris closed his eyes but in his mind he could still see the rocks and crashing waves at the bottom of the cliff. He felt his breath stop.

Then he heard a scream that seemed to be coming from his own throat.

But it was not his own scream. It was Fiona's.

He heard a dull thud and then felt Ross's grip on him loosen. Chris opened his eyes. The next thing he knew the whole cliff area behind him was flooded with light and he was blinded. He heard Steve crying softly, and he heard other voices, too. Fiona was sobbing, holding a large rock. And then his father was holding him, hugging him tightly.

"It's okay, it's okay," Paul kept repeating.

Through the tears in his eyes, Chris could see several policemen holding searchlights. One was handcuffing Ross. Standing with another policeman was old Angus. And Duncan.

Steve was free and was kneeling next to him. Paul grabbed Steve, too, and circled them both with his long arms.

"You're safe now," he said. "You're both safe."

Eleven

L ATER that evening, Chris and Steve sat
in front of the fireplace in the drawing
room back at castle Macgregor. Chris could tell
by the look on Steve's face that he had had
enough adventure for awhile.

The roaring fire in the big fireplace and
several cups of hot cocoa had helped the boys
stop shivering.

The police inspector was standing with Paul
and Duncan. Angus and Mary were talking
with a few of the police officers. The rest of the
officers had taken Captain Ross and Fiona
back to police headquarters in Inverness.

"A nasty business," said the police inspector,
a tall man named Johnstone. "We've had some
contact with this Captain Ross, as he calls
himself now. He's even spent some time in Her
Majesty's prison in Dartmoor for blackmail,
forgery, and assault with a deadly weapon.

He's not a pleasant character."

"You can say that again," said Steve, rubbing his bruised ribs where Ross had kicked him.

"How was he able to get Fiona mixed up in this?" asked Paul.

"Of course, we don't know the whole story yet," answered Inspector Johnstone. "But it seems he found out about the etching and the poem and decided he would trick Fiona into helping him get it. As you know, Ross can be very charming when he wants to be. Sad to say, Fiona fell in love with him."

Chris glanced at his father. Paul had taken a seat on the couch. He was staring blankly into the fire as the inspector talked about Fiona and Captain Ross.

"I'm partly to blame for that."

Duncan's deep voice startled the group. He had been silent until then. "It can be lonely up here. I've grown to like being alone. But Fiona never got used to it. And I wanted her to stay here and help me run the castle and estate. But there were very few people for her to spend time with. So when Ross came along, paying attention to her and charming her, it's not surprising that she fell in love with him. How was she to know that he was just using her to get at the treasure?"

"Do you think he ever really planned to

marry her?" asked Chris.

Duncan shrugged his shoulders. "I doubt it, lad. Ross doesn't strike me as the marrying type."

"Poor Fiona," Steve added. "Will she have to go to jail?"

"That'll be up to the police and the judges," answered Duncan.

"Well, she did knock Ross out with the rock, just when he was about . . . about . . . to push me over the edge," added Chris.

"I'm sure the police will take that into account," said Duncan.

Chris saw the sadness in his father's eyes as the inspector talked about whether Fiona would have to go to prison. Chris got up from his place by the fire and walked over and sat down next to Paul. "Don't worry, Dad," he whispered so that only Paul could hear. "We've still got each other."

Paul put his arm around Chris and pulled him close. "I know, Chris. I know." Chris saw that his dad's eyes were watery as he gazed into the blazing fire.

"Tell us how you found out where we were," said Steve. "You got there just in time!"

"When I heard you telling Paul about the cliff face and the map in the library that night," Duncan explained, "I guessed what

Ross and Fiona were up to. I had heard the legends about the poem and the treasure, but I didn't think they were true. When I heard you say that they had the poem, I decided to go to Inverness and do some checking on Ross. What I found out sent me to the police. And when I was talking to Inspector Johnstone earlier this evening, Paul suddenly showed up. We compared notes on what we knew and that was enough to get the police involved. We knew you might be in danger, so we took a police helicopter back to the castle.

"It was a hairy ride," added Paul. "With the fog and the wind and not knowing if you guys were safe, well, I'd rather go rafting down the Grand Canyon any day!"

"But how did you know that we were out at the ruined fort?" Steve asked.

"Ah, laddie," said Angus stepping forward, "do you remember the snapping twig you heard before you saw the hare jump out and run away? Well, that was me who made the noise."

"No way!" cried Chris.

Angus's old face crinkled with a smile. "Aye. The laird asked me to keep a sharp eye on the two of you while he was away in Inverness. He had a feeling that Fiona and Ross might try something—and they did!"

"Angus followed you part of the way, far enough to guess where you were going," Paul said. "Then he came back to wait for Duncan and the police. He led us right to you."

"But who put the note under our door?" asked Steve.

"That was Ross himself," answered Inspector Johnstone. "He slipped it under your door. We found a small piece of wood that he had jammed into the lock to keep you from getting out of your room right away. That gave him time to get back to the fort."

"What will happen to the treasure now?" Paul asked.

"Well," explained the inspector, "of course, we have to find it first. But with the excellent detective job that you boys did, we shouldn't have any trouble finding it—if it's really there after all these years. It will belong to the descendants of the original owners."

"You mean all the other lords who gave their treasure to the old laird of Macgregor Castle?"

The inspector nodded and said, "Yes, and there should be enough money for Laird Macgregor, too." He turned to Duncan. "You won't be needing to have any more groups here in Macgregor Castle, Laird Macgregor."

The group was quiet for a few minutes until

Inspector Johnstone said, "Well, perhaps it's time for us to think about getting back to Inverness—now that you're all safe and everything's calmed down."

Paul shook hands with the inspector. The boys thanked him and his men for saving their lives. Angus poked at the dying fire.

"Umm, Duncan," said Steve, walking up to the laird. "I guess we owe you an apology for all the things we've said about you. We were really wrong."

"Yeah," added Chris, joining him. "We're sorry. We were really stupid."

Duncan's hard face softened. "I accept your apologies, lads."

"It's just that we, uh, heard you and Fiona arguing one night and thought that it was about the treasure," explained Steve.

Duncan nodded and said, "I've told you about how I've come to enjoy the quiet life here. It's never been easy for me to open up the castle to visitors, even though I know I must to make ends meet. Fiona and I have been arguing about having paying visitors at Castle Macgregor. She wanted more and more groups here, and it was hard for me to accept. I understand now that she was trying to help me out with money problems. It was also her way of fighting the terrible loneliness she felt.

Even though we're related by blood, she and I are very different people. I'm not very good company and that was hard for her to accept."

The group got quiet after Duncan had spoken. The only sounds were the dry wood crackling in the fireplace and the wind blowing outside. A knock on the door startled all of them.

Angus opened it. It was the lawyer from San Diego.

"Hi," he said. "We were all just wondering what was going on. Is it okay if we come in?"

Paul looked around. Duncan shrugged. "Uh, sure. You might as well hear the whole story," sighed Paul.

The six guests filed in and took seats around the fire. Paul told them about the etching and poem, about Fiona and Ross, and about the rescue. When he finished, he held out his hands and said, "I'm really sorry for ruining your trip. I'll be glad to refund your money. I know it's been a disaster—a Disaster Unlimited."

"What are you talking about, Paul?" asked the lawyer. "This has been the trip of a lifetime! Staying in this fantastic castle, seeing the incredible scenery, and now a real-life mystery! This is my most exciting vacation ever!"

"And don't forget the phantom bagpiper!" cried another guest. "We even have a ghost."

They heard a soft chuckle from the

corner. It was Mary.

"Why, Angus Campbell! You should be ashamed of yourself for not telling them!"

All eyes turned toward the old couple. Angus smiled sheepishly.

"Umm, what Mary means is that, well, the bagpiper isn't exactly a phantom, In fact, *I'm* the bagpiper. It's my hobby!"

Everyone roared with laughter.

"You see, the Highland bagpipes are so loud and powerful that I have to go someplace far away to play them. I like to practice up in the tower. That way, if I sound awful, people won't want to throw me and my bagpipes in the loch!"

They all clapped and shouted. "We're going to tell all our friends about this!" one woman said. "They'll be so jealous! It's like being in a mystery novel."

Paul looked around and laughed. "Well, uh, I wish I could say I planned everything to happen this way. But I really can't take credit for the mystery. You'll have to thank the kids for that." Everyone laughed some more.

"Really, Paul," said the lawyer from San Diego, "the only thing missing was a chance to photograph the Loch Ness monster."

"Wait a minute!" Steve screamed. "My pictures! Angus, did you get them developed?"

"Why, yes. Yes I did," he answered. "I forgot

to give them to you in all the excitement. I'll go get them." The old man left the room. While he was gone, Steve and Chris explained to everyone about the night they saw the mysterious thing on the loch.

After what seemed like an hour to Steve, Angus came back with an envelope. He handed it to Steve, who ripped it open. He pulled out the photos with trembling hands as everyone crowded around him. Even Duncan seemed excited.

"Let me see!" yelled Chris. "Let me see!"

Steve held the photos under a lamp. Everyone was shouting and pushing to get a look. Steve was so excited he could barely look at them. His hand was shaking so much that Chris said, "Hold it still, darn it! We can't see it!"

Chris grabbed the photo and studied it.

"Oh no!" he cried, holding the photo so everyone could see.

The picture was reddish, since Steve had shot into the setting sun. The light was bad and the image was out of focus. In the middle of the dark loch was a long, fuzzy shape that could have been almost anything—a stick, a bird, or a prehistoric creature.

"You really can't tell what it is," said the San Diego lawyer, his voice thick with disappointment.

Steve groaned when he looked at the

picture. The second one was just as bad. He threw the photos down on the table. "Nuts! I wasted the chance of a lifetime!"

Chris put his arm on Steve's shoulder. "Ahh, it wasn't your fault. It was too dark and too far away."

"Chris is right," added Duncan. "No one could have taken a good picture under those circumstances."

"I guess we'll never know if the monster is out there or not," said Paul. "Maybe it should remain a mystery."

"Aye," said Angus softly. "Perhaps Paul is right, lads. Maybe there are some things we just aren't meant to know."

"I guess you're right," muttered Steve.

Then, floating on the night air, from somewhere out over the deserted moor, came a sound. It was the familiar wail that they had heard before.

An eerie hush fell over the room. Not a person moved.

"Listen!" whispered Chris. "Do you hear it?"

"It's the bagpiper!" said one of the guests. "The one that means the monster is near!"

"B-b-but Angus is here, with us!" said Steve in a choking voice. "Who's playing the bagpipes?"

Everyone in the darkened room looked in the direction of Loch Ness. But no one spoke a word.